REFORM SCHOOL
Cinderella

A NOVEL BY
FRANK CONNIFF

Published By
Podhouse 90 Press
ISBN: 978-0-578-49903-1

First Edition, 2019

Design, Typesetting and Cover Design by Len Peralta

*Dedicated to all fictional characters, in gratitude
for the great help they give to nonfictional characters.*

CHAPTER ONE

You have to believe me when I tell you that my dad is not as scary as he looks.

Honestly, he's not. Deep down, he's a nice guy and you'd like him if you got to know him. It's just that he hates it when people try to get to know him.

He's a police detective, and a very good one. He's not the least bit corrupt, nor does he engage in police brutality. But there's something about the way his eyes burn like scalding black coffee that gives suspects the impression that he could go full-psycho at any moment. It's a gift.

Look, I'm not saying my dad isn't scary. But my original point stands: he's not as scary as he looks.

And his basic look – a cold, pale face, prematurely-grey crew-cut hair, thick slab of a body that serves as its own armor – gives off the impression that he would be the top model if they ever put out a "Guys You Don't Want To Mess With" calendar.

I don't look like my dad in the least bit, and being a sixteen-year-old girl and all, that is something I am deeply grateful for. Also, I know for a fact that people are not afraid of me, because in most instances they don't even notice me in the first place.

It's not that I'm necessarily unattractive. I might even be pretty, not in a leading lady kind of way, but in a best-friend-of-the-leading-lady kind of way, or at least in a best-friend-of-the-best-friend-of-the-leading lady kind of a way.

The thing is, I don't fantasize about being prettier than I am, I fantasize about having a best friend. As I navigate the hallways and classrooms of my school, it's like I'm wearing a charisma-free fragrance. My everyday body contortion — head down, shoulders hunched, feet moving fast — is the only dance we shy people know.

But I try not to focus on my looks. Ultimately, a person's appearance shouldn't matter. It's the inner-self that is meant to be the true source of anxiety and depression.

I'm not sure if dad is aware of the stress that comes from walking the mean streets of a suburban high school, but he does try to shield me from the dangers of his job. He doesn't want me to worry, so he never talks to me about his police work. He doesn't talk about much of anything with me; that's just the way he is. But recently he brought his work home with him, or I should say his work arrived on our front yard. So I was a witness when he tried to apprehend a suspect, and I don't think he'd contradict me if I said this was the weirdest suspect he had ever encountered.

This guy was walking down the street on our block in the middle of the night holding an iPad that looked normal enough, except that it had a mega-bright screen that illuminated our neighborhood like a searchlight. Every house he walked by became bathed in light. Nobody noticed it at first because everyone was asleep.

Except my dad. And me.

Dad doesn't sleep much. He's usually too wound up from chasing down criminals all day. So Dad noticed the bright beam of light as it passed our house.

I don't sleep much either. I have insomnia, but I don't mind it because I like to stay up and read. I enjoy all sorts of books — historical romance, futuristic romance, fantasy romance, vampire romance, zombie romance, sci-fi romance, romance/romance — as you can see, I have a wide variety of literary interests. I also like to read history and biographies and books about popular culture in all its forms. And even though I'm a junior in high school, I still like to read fairy tales on occasion. If I'm too old, or too young for something, that's the sweet spot in terms of stuff that interests me.

And because I read so much, I tend to express myself more like a grown-up than a teenager. I've been told that I'm smart for my age and articulate beyond my years, which is another way of saying I'm friendless and have no social skills.

I guess the stress from spending all day being a social outcast at school is one of the things that keeps me up at night, so when the harsh bright light from that iPad screen scanned our house, I was wide awake and able to watch through my second floor bedroom window as dad went outside to investigate.

On the sidewalk in front of our lawn, dad approached the suspect, who was engrossed in whatever was on that computer screen and was completely lost in thought.

Now, my dad sees every human being on the planet as a potential suspect, but this guy looked like he could be an instructor at Suspect U. He had a genuine ogre vibe about him; I mean he totally looked like a real life mythical creature who happened to be carrying an iPad. He was big and fat and hairy. He was wearing some kind of weird flowery double-breasted uniform that made it look like he worked as a parking valet at a swanky hotel in the middle of a renaissance festival. It was the kind of outfit you'd get made fun of for wearing, unless you were as huge and threatening looking as this guy.

"Excuse me, what are you doing here in the middle of this street in the middle of the night?" Dad asked him.

The suspect did not answer. He just growled.

"Can I see some ID please?"

More growling, and then the suspect lunged forward and pushed Dad hard, sending him flying backwards. He hit a parked car, shattering the glass and setting off all the car alarms on the street.

The one good thing about all the noise was that it muted the sound of my scream. I knew my dad had many encounters with suspected law-breakers, but this was the first time I had ever seen him in action. It wasn't exciting, it was upsetting.

Dad was shaken up, but he regained his bearings right away, then embraced the ogre, but not in an affectionate way, more in a I'm-putting-you-in-a-headlock-and-cuffing-you-and-talking-you-downtown-you-lousy-dirtbag way.

Lights in the windows of the other homes on the street began to turn on.

Our quiet residential block just outside Minneapolis now resembled a noisy outdoor wrestling arena.

Dad is a big guy, but Mr. Ogre was even bigger. So it was cool AF that Dad was kicking this dude's ass. It wasn't long before he was moments away from cuffing and arresting him.

But then the Ogre disappeared. Literally. Into thin air. No kidding, he just up and vanished from dad's chokehold.

I don't think they train you at the police academy for this sort of thing.

Our neighbors, in bathrobes, pajamas and boxer shorts, began emerging from their homes moments after the suspect disappeared. They didn't see what had happened, and it looked to them like my dad was drunk or out of his mind or something.

But I saw it all and I knew that an unexplainable phenomenon had just occurred.

"Everything's okay," Dad announced to our neighbors as he stood up. "There's nothing to see here. Go back to bed."

Our neighbors did as they were told because, believe me, when my dad orders you to do something, there's a good chance you're going to do it. A million loud verbal altercations had given his working-class Minnesota accent a tracheotomy. If asbestos could talk, it would probably sound like my dad.

And there really was nothing to see, in more ways than one.

That's why my dad was so confused.

I was not used to seeing him in such a bewildered state. He is usually certain about things, at least as far as police work is concerned. When it comes to being a dad, on the other hand, well, there is some confusion involved. Parenthood does not come naturally for him, and this was especially the case after my mom died.

But Mom's disappearance from our lives, as painful at it was, was easy to explain. Cancer. Illness. Basic tragic nature of existence. That sort of thing. Dad was able to account for everything that happened; it was all there in the paper work and he was able to file it away, officially and emotionally.

But when a guy vanishes into complete nothingness as you're arresting him, that's a little hard to describe on an arrest report.

Dad came back into the house and sat down on our living room couch, pretty shaken up. As I walked down the stairs, I could see that he was thinking hard and trying to make sense of what had just happened.

"Dad, can I get you anything?" I said.

"Why are you awake, honey?" he said. "You should be in bed. You have school tomorrow."

"I know. I just wanted to make sure you're okay."

"I'm fine," he said.

That's what he always says. "I'm fine" is his stock response to everything. He said it right after Mom's funeral. He said it that time when he had pneumonia. And he was saying it now that a suspect had vanished from his hands as he was arresting him. But in this case it was more obvious than usual that the whole "I'm fine" response didn't hold.

I know that my dad loves me, but he would never do something out of the ordinary, like for instance, say it out loud, I just know he does. But the thing that he really loves, that he worships more than anything, is The Law. He loves The Law in all its forms. But this ogre's disappearance defied every law of physics and science and jurisprudence, and I'm sure there aren't any ordinances on the books that address the legality of public invisibility. As a detective, Dad is always in search of an explanation for things. Or, more precisely, a logical explanation. But there was no logical explanation for this. And that explained why he was so out-of-sorts.

He suddenly jumped up from the couch.

"I've got to go down to the station and look through mug shots," he said.

Looking through mug shots is something Dad does for fun, but in this case there was a real urgency to it.

"You stay inside and keep all the doors locked, understand?" he said.

He gave me his hardest, most severe look. This is the look he gives when he wants to create the impression that disobeying him is a felony offense. I mean, even when he says stuff like "Happy Birthday, darling," it can sound like a threat, but in this case I could tell he meant business.

"Yes, of course, dad," I said.

He rushed out the door. I locked it behind him, and then I got ready to go back into bed with the book I was reading, *Vampire's Weekend with Zombies*, which is a kind of Romeo and Juliet story that I assumed would be set in a dystopian rain-soaked Seattle, but the twist is that it's set in a dystopian rain-soaked Tacoma. Anyway, before I even went upstairs to start reading, I heard our front door being unlocked. Dad had returned.

He was holding my iPad. "Laura, you left this out on the lawn. At first I thought it might be the iPad that the suspect was carrying, but then I investigated and saw that it's yours."

He handed me the tablet and sure enough, it was mine: my home page photo of Robot Eleanor Roosevelt was proof of that. (It was from a historical sci-fi graphic novel I had read that wasn't very good, but I liked the image.)

"This isn't like you at all, Laura," Dad said. "You've got to be more careful. Remember how you bugged me and bugged me and bugged me until I finally bought the iPad for you. And this is how you treat it?"

I had asked him once, explaining that it would help with my schoolwork, and he immediately purchased it for me. That was his interpretation of me bugging and bugging him to buy it for me. But before I could say anything, he abruptly turned around, rushed outside, and locked the door behind him. I was as surprised at myself as he was for leaving the iPad on the lawn because he was right — it wasn't like me to be so careless.

But wait a minute, wasn't I reading a book on my iPad in my room just now before all this commotion started? How did it get out on the lawn? What the hell was going on?

I went back to my room, and my iPad was still on the nightstand next to my bed. So the one I was holding that my dad had just handed to me wasn't mine. But when I typed in my password, it opened up, and it had all my stuff stored on it, including my *Vampire's Weekend with Zombies* fan fiction. (I can't even believe I'm admitting that I write fan fiction. Yikes!)

So I opened the iPad by my bed, but it wasn't my iPad anymore, it had a picture of that hideous Ogre dude on it, so it was his. But how did his iPad and my iPad get switched?

I didn't dwell on that question because suddenly I had bigger things to worry about. The bright light that had gotten our attention in the first place was once again glowing from the computer screen, completely engulfing me.

What came next was incredibly strange, not the type of thing you'd expect to ever happen, especially on a school night.

10

CHAPTER TWO

I was now completely engulfed in the light from the iPad, but after a moment, I began to see text on the screen. It was displaying one of the books in my Kindle app, but not *Vampire's Weekend with Zombies,* which is the book I had been reading before I was rudely interrupted by this whole magical-forces-beyond-our-understanding thing. The text came more sharply into view and I could see that the book was *Reform School Cinderella.*

Now, this was a book that appeared in a "recommended titles" list a few days earlier and had cost only 99 cents, so on a whim I had downloaded it. I've always liked the Cinderella story. As sophisticated as I like to think I am, I can be a real sucker for this kind of kid's stuff. So I bought the e-book. What did I have to lose, besides 99 cents?

I was intrigued by the title, and was expecting maybe a cool young adult novel, or better yet, a subversive immature adult novel. This, however, was clearly a children's picture book written in rhyme. It looked to me like the type of book I had outgrown years ago, but I had already spent my money, so I gave it a read:

Once upon a time in a far away place
There lived a wretched girl, a sad and hopeless case
Her name was Cinderella, so you will not be surprised
That she lived with her step-siblings and was thoroughly despised
They kept her dressed in rags and locked behind closed doors
They made her cook and clean and other thankless chores

Okay, so far this was pretty much what I expected, nothing out of the ordinary. I already knew this story by heart, and the rhyming didn't make it any less childish. It inspired my own rhyme to appear inside my head:

Why are you reading this, don't you already know
You outgrew this kind of crap many years ago

But I had already spent my 99 cents, so I kept reading:

Then one day the Prince announced to all that he
Would host an awesome ball, so please RSVP
Only fair maidens could attend, the Prince had to insist
So of course Cinderella was crossed off the guest list
She felt so low and sad to be denied this dream
It sure did not do much to lift her self-esteem
But came the night of the ball, it was really somethin'
When her Fairy Godmother came and transformed a pumpkin

Okay, you know what? "Somethin'" is not really a word and even it were, it doesn't rhyme with "pumpkin", and at the age of sixteen I was about fifteen years too old for this junk anyway so I would have deleted the book, if I didn't already have a strict policy of always reading books to the end.

(Instituting strict policies about what I read and watch and how I read and watch it is my way of bringing form and structure to the many hours I spend by myself. I sometimes think I'm either on my way to becoming a Trappist Monk, or the Unibomber.)

Anyway, the picture book story continued:

Cinderella was the belle of the Prince's fancy ball
He danced with her all night, preferring her to all
But when she went to the bathroom, her step-sisters both did seek
To try to beat up Cinderella before she took a leak

Wait a minute, I thought. I wasn't expecting that to happen. I had never read a version of the Cinderella story that had a girl-fight or a bathroom break. This book was starting to get interesting, or at least less boring.

Cinderella fought back and gave as good as she got
But she had to flee the ball 'cause things were getting hot
She left behind a slipper as a lingering reminder
The Prince tortured and killed in his search to somehow find her

What? The Prince was a torturer and killer? Who wrote this book, Dick Cheney?

Finally he found her and the foot perfectly fit
But a defiant Cinderella was having none of it
She said she wouldn't marry him, that he could go to hell
So she was arrested and imprisoned in a well padded cell

That's it. That's the end of the book! Needless to say, it was not what I expected. I liked that the Cinderella portrayed in this version was kind of a badass, but to be honest, I didn't enjoy the story. It was a bit of a downer.

Right after I got to the words, "The End," I noticed there was a link below the text that said, "RATE THIS BOOK."

Well, I had nothing better to do, so I clicked the link. It took me to a page that had the usual ratings system, one to four stars. As someone who enjoys reading, and maybe would even like to be a writer myself one day (I'm still too young to decide exactly which profession I'm going to suffer at when I'm an adult), I decided to be supportive of whomever wrote this book (there was no author listed, so the writer might be even shyer than I am, which endeared him or her to me). I saw that nobody had left a rating or any comment, and it looked like I was the only person who had purchased the book, and then I really felt bad for the author, so in the interest of some future undefined karma that might come my way, I clicked the four stars icon.

Now here it was a few days after I had read the book, and that karma had arrived in my life, but it didn't seem like it was the good kind of karm because I knew that somehow, my interaction with this book was responsible for the bright light shooting from the iPad that was now engulfing me.

I had no doubt the Cinderella book was the cause of this because suddenly the text from the book was all over the walls of my room like some kind of rhyming graffiti.

It was as if everything inside our house was being x-rayed. I could now see the couch, the chairs, the coffee table, and all the other furniture, but I could also somehow see a different world inside and beyond the furniture, if that makes any sense (I'm fully aware, it doesn't).

It was like I could see the skeletal insides of inanimate objects, and it was as if those inanimate objects where alien creatures from another planet with intricate bone structures that no human has ever seen before. I hope this doesn't sound too weird. (I'm fully aware, it does.)

I was tempted to throw the computer tablet down on the floor and maybe even stomp it to pieces, because what was happening to me was what I imagined it would feel like to get a cat-scan in a giant lava lamp in the middle of Coachella.

But I didn't stomp on the iPad because I was detecting a beeping noise coming from our basement, and that beeping noise didn't start until the bright light from the iPad had begun, so I was compelled to investigate and see if I could possibly find out what was going on.

I followed the beeping sound towards our basement, all the while trying to not let my senses be overwhelmed by the translucent abstract expressionism that was revealing itself inside everyday objects like doorknobs and end tables and reading lamps.

I wished my mom were still around even more than I usually did. She always seemed to have a sense of a world beyond our world. She wasn't religious or anything like that; she worked in Human Resources and was tightly tethered to the real world, which made it way too real when she was abruptly taken from the world through no fault of her own. But she always said that there was more to our existence than we could possibly end, and that the landscape of imagination was an actual tangible we could seek out and have access to. Dad, whose life is devoted ulating hard evidence, was not on the same page with her when it

14

came to this kind of stuff, so if Mom were still here she would be the one who might have some kind of insight into all this otherworldly insanity I was witnessing. Or she'd comfort me with hot chocolate and send me to bed. Either way, I wished she were still around.

I don't want to say that my mom had paranormal qualities, but she was able to make my dad smile and even laugh on occasion, and since then I've never met anyone in the known universe who is capable of that, so she certainly did have extraordinary powers.

Ever since Mom died, Dad doesn't really do the happiness thing anymore. So maybe that's why I was moving towards the unknown rather than away from it. This small suburban home of ours just outside Minneapolis was a house of depression, made that way by my grief-stricken dad and aided and abetted by his equally grief-stricken not to mention severely geeky and socially inept daughter, so a possible rip in the space/time continuum within our home was, to me at least, a welcome change of pace.

As I continued down to our basement, amid melting walls and a staircase that seemed like a an escalator moving up and down at the same time, I started thinking about Gil Davis, this senior who goes to my school. Now, even though some crazy stuff was happening at that moment, it wasn't altogether weird that I was thinking about Gil Davis because I think about him all the time.

Most of my thoughts about him are philosophical, like for instance — If Gil Davis doesn't ever notice me, am I even real? Do I even exist? So far the answer I've come up with is, hell if I know. He's never looked at me, much less smiled or said hi, so I really have to question whether I'm even a thing.

Now, make no mistake, I am my own person, and I do not need another human being to validate my existence. Which is one of the reasons why my existence sucks so hard.

God knows I've tried to make human contact (sort of). The other day in the school cafeteria, Gil Davis was walking towards where I was sitting, and it occurred to me that if I looked at him, there might be the slight possibility that he would look back. This seemed a long shot, an emotional science experiment, but I wanted to give it a try.

Of course, I chickened out. He walked right past me and I never even lifted my head to meet his eyes until it was too late. In a way, I was relieved, because what if I had looked at him and what if he had looked back and what if someone else had seen me make eye contact with him and then everyone in the school would have known that I liked him, and I would have been exposed as a person who likes another person, and I would never have been able to live down the shame of that.

Anyway, I continued walking downstairs and followed the beeping noise to our basement. I don't spend a lot of time down there, except to use the washer and dryer, which at this moment looked like they were both spin-drying comic book splash pages. There's not much else in the basement except a ratty couch and a boiler. Dad likes to sit in the basement on that couch, drinking beer and brooding in the dark. It relaxes him, I guess. Sometimes he watches the clothes spinning in the dryer because he says it's better than what's on TV. My dad has issues, I know, but like I said, once you get past the tragic intensity of his deeply troubled psyche, he's not a bad guy.

The beeping was coming from the brick wall opposite the couch. I pointed the light from the iPad at the wall, and it revealed what I can only describe as an entire universe behind the wall. There was a tunnel that seemed to go on forever. It looked like it was maybe a portal into another world, but I don't think anybody knew about it. Otherwise, I'm sure it would have had some effect on the property value of our house.

And if our landlord knew about this tunnel, he would have no doubt tried to exploit it for profit, because he's a jerk. He wouldn't pay for repairs to water damage after a flood until finally my dad did his bad cop/worse cop routine on him. Then the plumber was at our house within the hour, but it should never have to come to that.

I moved closer to the wall, and I continued to keep the light from the iPad pointed at it. The closer I got, the more it illuminated the wall, and suddenly it looked like the plaster was cracking. Layers upon layers of wall began flipping away, and as each wall flipped away, another infinite universe was revealed. But since it was all happening on an intergalactic realm beyond the scope of human understanding, it wasn't causing any kind of mess in our basement, so at least the stupid landlord wouldn't be able to take this cosmic occurrence out of our damage deposit.

The long tunnel had a brilliant multi-colored glow to it, like an aurora borealis that had been put in storage. I knew instinctively that if I took one step forward, I would be entering an uncharted world from which there might be no return.

But I was all hyped up now, and I didn't think I could fall asleep anyway. So the idea of stepping into another dimension in the middle of the night was appealing to me, although I know now that I should have called my dad and asked for permission.

But I stepped forward, and the stress and turmoil I was about to endure as a result of this action was not something I would wish on my worst enemy. Or even my best enemy. Not to be a drama-queen, but I doubt if anyone has ever suffered as much just because they read and recommended a dumb children's book.

CHAPTER THREE

After walking a few feet into the tunnel, I began to feel a sort of motion sickness, but I wasn't dizzy or nauseous. It was more like the world around me was hyperventilating, but within the tunnel it felt normal, except that it wasn't normal for me to feel normal in such an abnormal setting.

I don't know how long I walked. Time didn't stand still so much as fidget in one place. As I moved forward, I passed other passageways that led to other vortexes or universes or black holes or God knows what. But the beam coming from my computer tablet was like a homing device and it strongly indicated that I should continue in the direction I was going.

Out of the corner of my eye, I could briefly see into passageways to other dimensions, and the quick images I viewed seemed oddly familiar to me. At the end of one hallway, I saw what looked like a bunch of Vampires and Zombies. They could have been characters from *Vampire's Weekend with Zombies*. They were kissing and making out, just like they did in the book, but it was much less romantically appealing to see it happen in person. I'm sorry, but I just don't think the undead and the walking dead should engage in public displays of affection, although I don't seem to have a problem with them eating each other's flesh and sucking each other's blood, so obviously I'm the one with hang-ups.

Down another passageway, a moody looking kid was walking down the streets of what might have been New York City, except with vintage cars from the 1950s. I had recently read *Catcher In The Rye*, (I saw a copy in Gil Davis' back pocket, then read the whole thing that night) and this kid matched the description of Holden Caulfield, but I didn't want him to see me because I had no doubt he would think that people who hang out in trans-dimensional vortexes are a bunch of phonies.

Then I took a sideways glance at another passageway, and I saw a woman in nineteenth century garb jumping in front of a train. This was weird because recently, over a period of several weeks, I had finally finished *Anna Karenina*. (Spoiler Alert: In the end, she jumps in front of a train, although the story deals with other issues besides public transportation.) The book is romantic and tragic so of course I loved it.

I guess it made sense that this otherworldly tunnel I had entered was somehow related to literature because a book had instigated the whole journey in the first place. But what made even more sense was that I had lost my freaking mind. Regardless, I focused on the radar beam from my computer and kept moving forward.

Eventually I arrived at what looked like a steel wall. As soon as I was standing in front of the wall, the tablet that I clutched in my hand started vibrating. At first it was like a regular cell phone vibration but then it felt like an electric shock and it hurt, so I let go of the device.

But it didn't drop to the floor; instead the iPad flew out of my hand and attached itself to the steel wall, and then began moving in a circular fashion, as if it was wiping dust from the wall. And as the "dust" cleared, what I saw looked like a plastic bullet-proof window, with a distressed girl staring at me from the other side.

She was dressed in an orange jump suit and she looked like she hadn't been in the sun for a long, long time. So maybe she was from Minnesota, just like me. But in addition to being pale, she was also a bit emaciated. And yet her determined look of urgency made her seem strong, not weak.

In her hand she held an old-fashioned non-digital type of paper tablet.

The writing on it was a kind of ancient, old English font, the type you'd see on a scroll in a Robin Hood movie. Through the glass, I could just barely make out the words, "Hold down the # key on your computer keypad."

I pried the tablet from the wall and did so. A rectangular razor beam shot out from the iPad and quickly and silently disintegrated the window. I had no idea my tablet had the capacity to do such a thing, and I assumed that this one application had used up all of my storage space. The force of the lazar left a big opening in the glass, big enough to walk through.

The girl put her finger to her lips.

"If we get caught we could be in big trouble," she whispered.

We?

"Where am I? What's going on?" I whispered back.

"You've opened up a trans-dimensional tunnel to an enchanted storybook world," she said.

"Uh…cool?" I replied.

"Not really," she said. "Right now we're standing in the Fairy Tale Reformatory, but thanks to you, I'm busting out of here right now!"

She seemed like a person that didn't fit in with her surroundings. This made me instantly like her. But there was something I had to say:

"Here's the thing: I'm the daughter of a law enforcement official, so I don't think he'd approve of me aiding and abetting a fugitive from a correctional facility."

"If you help me break out of here, I will be your friend forever!" she said.

The idea of having a forever friend was appealing, but still, I was not one to help a fugitive criminal; it's just not the way I was brought up. However, this fugitive criminal was not from our world, but from an alternate universe, which probably had different laws and different standards of justice. Isn't it just my luck that when I finally meet someone who wants to be my friend, all sorts of legal and moral ramifications come up?

But in the midst of weighing the pros and cons of helping this girl, I heard a clicking sound.

I looked up and saw a scary looking witch with some sort of rusty old-timey musket rifle that she was pointing at both of us. Her weapon looked like it was from the American Revolutionary War, so by her standards it was probably cutting-edge technology.

Look, I know I shouldn't prejudge this lady and say she was a witch just because her hair was chaotic and filthy, and her face had a million pockmarks, and her nose looked like a chewed up breadstick, and… Okay, you know what, I'm sorry, but there was no getting around it – she was the most witchy-looking person I had ever seen!

And she was wearing a drab institutional militaristic uniform that looked like it was straight off the rack from the Banality of Evil collection.

"Who the hell are you?" she said.

"Oh, uh, don't mind me," I said. "I'm not of your world."

"So if I pull this trigger and blow your brains out, it won't happen in this world?"

It was rhetorical question; nevertheless, I put my hands up. The other girl's hands were already up. She had a look of resignation that seemed to indicate this kind of thing happened to her a lot.

The scary witch/guard/whatever gestured with her gun for me to walk towards her and I did. She then took my iPad from me. This was upsetting because, as you know, my dad was already annoyed with me because he thought I had been careless with it, and I knew that telling him it was confiscated by a hideous gun-toting witch from The Land That Reality Forgot was not going to cut it with him.

We were marched down a long corridor that had all the charm and vibrancy of a Department of Motor Vehicles office.

"By the way," I said to my fellow prisoner as we continued walking. "My name is Laura."

"Nice to meet you," she said. "I'm Cinderella."

CHAPTER FOUR

Cinderella? Wow!

As we've already established, I had heard of her, I even read a few books about her, and in the most recent book I read, she ended up locked in an institution, so it made sense that this was the Cinderella from that particular book.

Normally my having just read a book about her would have been a good opening for a conversation, but since we were both being led at gunpoint to what in all likelihood was certain doom, this didn't seem to be the time to talk about her career or ask for an autograph. She was the first storybook character I had ever met in person, but I was too busy trying not to faint from fear to appreciate this exciting moment in my life.

She was exactly what you'd expect Cinderella to look like, except more bedraggled, like a beautiful celebrity being photographed by TMZ while coming out of an after-hours nightclub at six in the morning.

While keeping the gun trained on us, the witchy guard led us to a supply closet manned by an equally witchy looking female custodian. I would soon find that all of the women who worked in this place had gone with the witchy look and run with it. Good for them, that's their choice, I don't judge, but I think that if at least one or two of them had decided against embracing a middle-aged Manson Family vibe, it might have helped calm my nerves, although probably not by much.

"We're going to need an extra straitjacket," our guard said.

The unpleasant result of this exchange was that I ended up in a padded room wearing a very uncomfortable straitjacket (I doubt if they come in a comfortable size, and I know this must have been purely psychological, but I swear that the minute the buckles on my jacket were securely tied I had a desperate need to scratch my nose).

I was sitting on the floor across from Cinderella, who was flailing about as she tried to free herself from the matching garment she was wearing.

"Have they put you in a straitjacket before?" I asked.

"Millions of times."

"Were you ever able to free yourself?"

"Not without a magic incantation. But unfortunately I don't seem to have one of those handy right now."

I tried not to cry. In school, I had never even been in detention, and I was normally so quiet and incognito that I was never noticed long enough to get into any kind of trouble. If I was known at all, it was as a major wuss, and this was a reputation I had earned though the diligent application of interpersonal ineptness before, during, and after any kind of social situation.

We sat like this for what seemed like a long time, but it might have been just a few moments. Then the thick padded door opened and a male Sentry, wearing the same guard uniform that the lady witch wore, entered our cell.

(Just so you don't think I'm singling out our woman captor for her hideous looks, let me also point out that this male guard had a splotchy face that looked like dragon vomit.)

"You are both wanted in Dr. Strepgoat's office," he said.

"Dr. Strepgoat?" I whispered to Cinderella, as we were unhelpfully helped to our feet and lead out of our padded cell and down another damp, grey hallway. "Who is he?"

"The warden of this place, and my court-appointed therapist," she replied.

"Is he a good therapist?" I asked.

Cinderella shot me a look that left no doubt I was asking a stupid question.

We were taken to his office, and it was there that I got my first glimpse of Dr. Strepgoat. He was a short man wearing a long lab coat, so I didn't realize at first that he was half man/half goat. The upper half of his body was the man part. He had white whiskers and a completely bald head. His eyes were the blank color of nothing and he had a dour, judgmental look that made even a normally nonviolent person like myself want to punch him in the face.

The lower half of his body – the goat half – was the less repellant part, which is not to say it wasn't disgusting. He had a short stub of a tail that only partly covered up a part of his anatomy that no person who wants to hold down her lunch should ever see.

As was the case with almost everyone in this reformatory, except Cinderella, Doctor Strepgoat's story had not made it into the mainstream of fairy tale mythology. But I did get the chance to find out more about him later in the little-read storybook, *The Adventures of Doctor Strepgoat*. Here is that book in its entirety:

> *There once was a man without style or grace*
> *With a bad attitude you could see on his face*
> *He was mean and rude and never chipper*
> *A boring date and a lousy tipper*
> *But in the fairy tale world he had come to be*
> *A practitioner of licensed psychiatry*
> *And one of the patients he agreed to see*
> *Was possessed of a talent for sorcery*
> *He left his session on such a sour note*
> *That he turned his doctor into a half goat*
> *This made him more bitter and even more sore*
> *Especially when he took a crap on the floor*
> *But at his lowest point he was relieved when he*
> *Was appointed to head a Reformatory*
> *Where his pettiness has blossomed and grown*
> *And his career as a jerk has come into its own*

I can see why his storybook wasn't much of a success, and its failure was just one of the factors that gave him the bitterness and anger that was the foundation of his work in psychiatric therapy.

Cinderella and I sat in chairs facing him in his office, which had a thick carpet and wood paneling with a big picture window that looked out on a bucolic green meadow blocked by barbed wire. I got the impression that Dr. Strepgoat thought the barbed wire was the prettiest part of the view. This was the nicest scenery I had seen since I had arrived in this alternate universe and I still couldn't help but be depressed by it.

Cinderella and I were still in our straitjackets, so the warm earth tones of the room did nothing to improve our spirits.

"Well," Dr. Strepgoat said in a voice that reminded me of every mean-spirited authority figure I had ever met in my life. "You tunneled into here to help break Cinderella out…"

"That's not true!" Cinderella said.

"Did I ask you? Dr. Strepgoat snapped.

"Where was I? Oh yes…" he said, turning his attention back to me. "What part of the Enchanted Kingdom are you from?"

"Minnesota."

"I'm not familiar with that sector. What region is that in?"

"The cold one."

"Don't be impertinent with me, young lady!"

It has always been my experience that when you hear adults utter the phrase, "young lady," you are either being yelled at, or are about to be yelled at, or have just been yelled at.

"Look," Cinderella interjected. "She's not from around here. This is not her fault. She's innocent. Please let her go."

"A couple things, Cinderella," he said. "Firstly, I don't believe a word you're saying. And secondly, shut up!"

"But she's…"

"Why are you still talking?" he screamed.

He turned his angry face back towards me.

"Your attempt to try and break Cinderella out of here, after what she did to the Prince, says to me that you must be the lowest of criminals."

The lowest of criminals? Really? Me? Okay, I realized that in this new world, I was now considered a criminal. But the lowest? This was bad. I couldn't help myself, I panicked.

"My dad is a police officer!" I blurted out. "I have a deep respect for law enforcement. I would never do anything illegal!"

Cinderella's face turned a whiter shade of WTF. I think she thought I was about to sell her out, but it was just that every bone in my body was defibrillating with fear. It was as if I was being tased by my own psyche. Which is why the next thing I said was completely uncharacteristic of me.

"There's something you should know, doctor," I said.

"What's that?"

"My dad can beat up your dad. Which means he can sure as hell beat up you."

This did not endear me to Dr. Strepgoat. Cinderella smiled, which only pissed him off even more.

"I'm seriously considering putting in a requisition for a magic spell that would remove both of your mouths permanently," he said. Then he began a staring contest with me that he instantly won. Just as I turned away from him, he said, "You're going to tell me the truth, missy!"

It has been my experience that the only thing worse than hearing adults begin a sentence with, "young lady," is when they end it with, "missy."

It looked like he was about to bring some sort of hideous goat-justice down on both of our heads, and I braced myself. I was just as scared as ever, but because I had sort of stood up for Cinderella, I felt stronger, in a completely pointless way that wasn't going to do either of us any good.

But at that moment, the Sentry entered the room, marched over to Dr. Strepgoat, and whispered in his ear.

"What?!!!" Strepgoat barked, annoyed and upset by what he was hearing.

Cinderella and I were led out of the room.

"What's going on?" I whispered as we were taken away. "He was about to do something awful to us, and then it was like a reprieve from the Governor came through. What happened?"

"Only one explanation," Cinderella whispered back. "My Fairy Godmother."

Yes, I had heard of her. It looked like I was about to meet another celebrity.

CHAPTER FIVE

She was waiting for us in the visitor's room and she sure didn't look like any Fairy Godmother I had ever read about.

No big fluffy silken dress for her; instead she wore a tight black cat suit that hugged an athletic body. If she had achieved this physique with a magic wand, it was a four hundred pound one that she had lifted while climbing an elliptical beanstalk. Her cropped short hair was brown with grey streaks, and her eyes were weary yet alert, like a crossing guard on duty 24/7. She came off not like the whimsical eccentric of fairy-tale lore, but more like a hard-nosed military commando with an innate fashion sense. I was instantly intimidated, which I think is exactly what she was going for.

There was a long table in the middle of the room, one side for visitors, the other for inmates. At that moment she was the only visitor. We sat down opposite her.

She spoke to me in a voice that was soft yet rough, like cotton candy made from pork rinds. "Please tell me precisely how you obtained Agent O's e-book?" she said.

"Agent O?" I asked.

She showed me his picture. It was the Ogre that had disappeared while my dad was trying to arrest him outside our house. My first instinct was to ask if I could have the photo so I could give it to Dad — he had been looking for a mug shot of this guy — but I quickly realized that I was in no position to ask for evidence, however much the Minneapolis Police Department might need it.

I told her what had happened. She thought about it for a moment, then said, "This is bad, really bad."

"I know!" I said. "Now I'm stuck here."

"Actually, I was talking about Agent O. When your father was trying to arrest him, he must have inadvertently pushed a button on his belt that sent him into the outer reaches of the trans-dimensional vortex. And what I think happened is that in the midst of the struggle, he wasn't able to adjust his settings, so now he's floating randomly though the ether between worlds."

"Sounds painful," I said.

"It's certainly not fun."

"It's not fun being in this reformatory walking around in a straitjacket," I said. "I didn't ask to be here. All I did was click open an e-book and now I'm a prisoner. Not to be rude, but this sucks."

I felt like crying, but I didn't, because I wanted to appear strong in front of a couple of characters that might not even exist. What can I say, I'm a people-pleaser even when I'm not sure if the ones I'm trying to please are even people.

But saying what had happened out loud made the gravity of my situation all too real to me. This is why we never talk about painful stuff in the Midwest, and I made a mental note to never do it again.

"I admit, it is awful what has happened to you, and my organization is partly to blame," she said.

"Your organization?"

"I'm a top officer in a clandestine group of secret agents called the Fairy Tale Resistance. The enchanted world is filled with political oppression and human rights violations and we're trying to do something about it. In fact, from now on, please refer to me by my code name, Agent FG."

"Oh, you have a code name?" I said, my voice on the verge of collapsing. "That is so cool. My code name is, GET ME THE HELL OUT OF HERE!"

Now I was crying. It wasn't like me to carry on like this. But it also wasn't like me to be a political prisoner in a Storybook Dystopia, either.

"Please, try to calm down," Cinderella said, as soothingly as she could. "The Fairy Tale Resistance is a cool organization, in theory."

Then, her mood abruptly changed. "But on the other hand, they screw up all the time, and my so-called fairy godmother here hasn't performed a single useful bit of magic since the night of the ball, and all that abracadabra crap is what got me here in the first place."

"I've told you a million times," Agent FG said, in the same testy tone I've always heard adults use when their authority is questioned. "You think that just because I'm a Fairy Godmother I can merely wave a wand and make everything better. It doesn't work that way, There are all kinds of forces at play in the known world and the world beyond the known world. And Laura's dad trying to arrest Agent O didn't help matters any."

"My dad was just doing his job," I said. "Agent O was not cooperating, and my dad did not violate his constitutional rights. He just wanted to find out why he was lurking around our house at two in the morning."

"He was looking for you," Agent FG said.

"What?"

"More precisely, he was looking for the wi-fi signal from your iPad so he could transfer the trans-dimensional travel app from his tablet to your tablet, which he did successfully. Then he was going to gently guide you through the process of coming here and breaking Cinderella out of jail. But then your father interfered."

"That's all besides the point right now," Cinderella said. "The main thing is, the Fairy Tale Resistance has to get me out of here, and you need to help Laura as well. As my fairy godmother, it is your duty!"

"This girl has put our entire mission in jeopardy," Agent FG responded. "She may be a liability."

Now my fear, which I thought had been at maximum capacity, was turned up to eleven. I thought the Fairy Godmother, or Agent FG, or whatever damn name she went by, was supposed to be on our side.

"You're being completely uncool," Cinderella said. "Stop upsetting my friend and stop being totally useless."

"Useless?" Agent FG said, indignant. "I managed to mind-trick the guards and the folks who run this institution into allowing me to come here and visit. I have knowledge in the ways of enchantment and sorcery that will eventually enable us to dismantle this repressive regime and bring down the entire Fairy Tale kingdom!"

"I hope I'm not being out of line," I said. "But I've read a few books about Cinderella through the years, and you don't have much of a Fairy Godmother thing going on at all."

"Well, here's the thing, Laura. The book you read was the first accurate version of the Cinderella story," Agent FG said. "You were the only reader to buy it, and on top of that, you gave it a four star recommendation. That is why we sent Agent O to find you and guide you through the process of magically transporting you here. But because your father tried to arrest Agent O, and thus sent him spiraling into a vortex God-knows-where, you ended up coming here on your own and that is why everything went wrong when you arrived."

"So recommending that book was the trigger that set everything in motion that got me here?" I asked.

Agent FG nodded her head.

"In that case, I'm going to stop evaluating books altogether. I can't believe I'm in a world of trouble just because I recommended a book! I was also vilified in a Reddit sub-thread when I made a slightly negative comment about 'Twilight.' I just can't win!"

"Look, I'm sorry about what happened to you, but now that you're here, you can be of some help to us," Agent FG said. "Cinderella is the first subject of this regime to publicly shed light on the evil nature of the Prince's administration. He runs a fascist dictatorship where citizens of the fairy tale kingdom have no human rights. All of the girls in this reformatory were incarcerated without due processes. Yourself included."

"That is messed up," I said. "My dad works in the field of law enforcement, and although capturing criminals is his job, he's never locked up anyone without reading them their rights and giving them access to a court-appointed attorney. He would never stand for what's going on here."

"I hate to tell you this," Agent FG said. "But you're in a place where your father can't do anything to help you."

Wow. If this chick was trying to give me a pep talk, she was falling way short.

"Why did my four star recommendation of that book open up a trans-dimensional portal?" I asked "Why was I brought here?"

"We were hoping you could break Cinderella out of here. The plan was to have her escape into your world and then come back into our dimension through another portal that landed her outside the Reformatory. Since you are the only one who liked the book, or who even bothered to read the book, it was assumed that you would be sympathetic to our cause and would help us."

"Why can't you or Agent O just use magic to break her out?"

"That's what I keep asking her!" Cinderella said, shooting me a classic look of shared exasperation between two girls, something I had seen go on between other kids at school. I believe it's called camaraderie, and now that I was finally experiencing it, I wished it was happening under more normal circumstances.

"Magic can only do so much in a magical kingdom," Agent FG said. "We all exist within the confides of a pre-ordained narrative. Only by bringing in an outside force from an alternate world can that narrative be subverted and shattered. Does that make any sense?"

"Not in the least bit," I said, as politely as I could. I was starting to regret that I hadn't entered into a different storyline, something simpler and less stressful, like American Psycho.

"I just want to go home," I said in the weepy manner that had lately become my trademark.

"The Fairy Tale Resistance is prepared to help you," Agent FG said. "We will give you the resources you need both magical and otherwise. But first, you have to help us do something."

"What's that?" I asked.

"Assassinate the Prince."

CHAPTER SIX

Well, that was an anxiety-inducing meeting. And to be honest, I don't think participating in a plot to overthrow a monarchy is something my father would approve of. If he ever caught me assassinating a head of state, I'm pretty sure I'd be grounded.

Being imprisoned in this reformatory was much worse than being grounded, but at least I wasn't wearing the straitjacket anymore. I was issued an orange jumpsuit and told to go the cafeteria because it was now dinnertime. (If felt like early morning to me, but now that I was in an alternate universe the time zone was different I guess).

I didn't feel like eating. I was so nervous I barely had an apatite. Plus, going by what I've read in storybooks, I knew that fairy tale food wasn't very good. It's lumpy and overcooked and little too much on the cannibalistic side for my tastes.

When I arrived in the cafeteria I saw that this was an all-girl Reformatory. All the other prisoners were wearing the same identical orange jumpsuits, and they also wore the same look of pure, unconcealed disdain as they all glared at me. It seemed like despising me was a project that they had all worked on together. Being hated is awful, but it really sucks when it's the result of a team effort.

They all had a fairy-tale-character-in-decline look going on. I'm not knocking it; the dorky-girl-from-Minnesota thing I was into was no better, if you can even say that I had any kind of thing. Most of the inmates had wild, unruly hairstyles free from the burden of shampoos and conditioners.

Their eyes were bloodshot, and dental hygiene was not a trending topic in the magic kingdom.

If any of these girls had ever been fair maidens or princesses, those days were long behind them. Quite understandably, they were all in bad moods. The mean girls in my school would never dare mess with the mean girls in this place.

I was grateful that I was with Cinderella, but most of the other girls were looking at her with even more disapproval than they were showing towards me.

There was a line for food at a steam table. I wasn't hungry, but Cinderella got in line and I got in line behind her. Then another girl got behind me, and to my relief she sounded friendly.

"You're new here, huh? Welcome!" she said.

I turned and saw a girl that was outgoing yet off-putting. She had nervous energy, like a shaken soda can on the verge of exploding. Almost everyone in this place had bad complexion, but her skin was downright crispy.

"I'm Lunchabelle," she said. "Nice to meet you."

Before we go any further, you'd better read the Lunchabelle storybook. Like just about everyone else in the reformatory except Cinderella, her story is not widely known in our world. Most of my fellow prisoners were storybook characters who for one reason or another had never caught on with the general public. But Lunchabelle's story might give you some insight into her behavior:

There once were two kids, nothing special to see
Who lived in a gated community
Not far from a village, just on the outside
Where hungry witches were known to reside
And that was a problem for this girl and boy
Because they were the kind of meat that famished freaks enjoy
So if you wanted tasty tots sumptuous and rare
Lunchabelle and Lunchabill were your bill of fare
And so one day when they were lost in the woods
A ravenous witch thought they had the goods

33

She planned to eat them in a most gruesome way
And save the leftovers for the next day
But the kids were clever and their fortunes turned
When they threw her in the oven and she burned and burned
The kids' lives were saved and they won the day
But the juvenile court didn't see it that way
They were accused of murder, a capital offense
Even though they pleaded self-defense
They were going to be jailed for a long time
So the brother accused his sister of the crime
He turned state's evidence and sold her out
Sending her to to jail while he's out and about
Now she's locked away and so dearly wishes
That she wasn't cursed to be so darn delicious

Like a lot of the storybooks about the characters in this reformatory, Lunchabelle's story was pointless and gross, and thus is not an immortal beloved tale read by parents to their children. But like I said, she seemed nice, so I shook her hand, which had a film of grease on it. Immediately after we shook I wanted to wipe my palm on my jumpsuit but I didn't for fear that it might offend her.

"Don't even think about it!" she said.

"What?"

"I know what you're thinking, but you are not eating me. Understand?"

"Yes, of course," I said.

"She's a little paranoid," Cinderella said to me. "Understandably so. I mean, I'm not a cannibal, but look at her! She seems way more edible than the crappy food they serve in this dump."

Cinderella had a point. I would never, ever eat another human being, but Lunchabelle had the kind of smell that made you order Kentucky Fried Chicken against your better judgement, so I knew I'd better be careful around her.

But I didn't have time to think about this, because suddenly I felt something hit me from the side, something hard and thick that knocked me to the ground.

When my head stopped pounding long enough for me to open my eyes, I saw a granite monument to nastiness looking down at me, a girl with empty eyes that were a factory window to a pitiless soul. I'm saying that she didn't give off a good first impression.

Her sub-freezing face should have sent a chill down my spine, but it didn't, because I think I was experiencing spinal nerve damage.

Her hair was the harshest thing about her. It came down below her shoulders, and was the color of a federal courthouse. It looked to me like it was completely made of brick and mortar, a conclusion which, it turned out, was not far off the mark.

"That's Concretia," Cinderella said as she helped me to my feet. "She suffered a witch's spell that turned her hair to concrete, but I'm sure you read all about that in a storybook."

No, I hadn't read that story. Her storybook had flopped in the earthly realm. The only famous character in this place was Cinderella, and everyone seemed to be holding that against her.

And so, since I'm sure you haven't read it either, here is Concretia's storybook:

There once was a girl with such golden curls
She was the envy of all the girls
Her hair was curly and silky and soft
And it went to her head, sending her ego aloft
Her hair was lush and took up lots of space
And when she bragged about it, she was so in your face
It got on people's nerves and made them annoyed
So a resentful witch's spell was employed
Her hair was turned from stylish and slick
Into a giant slab of concrete brick
Her scary new look caused her such alarm
That she used her new 'doo to do bodily harm
Now she's locked away feeling nothing but dread
With a heavy heart and a heavier head

Her hair is a menace to the world's population
Because it's a building code violation

As you can see, there is reason to sympathize with Concretia, but it was hard to like her because she didn't like me. I know this, because she said, "I don't like you."

She started to swing her Stonehenge of a head towards me again, but Cinderella blocked her path.

"Leave her alone!" Cinderella said. "Anyone that wants to mess with the new girl has to come through me first!"

She said this directly to Concretia, but she was addressing everyone. She stood with her fists in a combative stance, ready for a fight, maybe even hoping for one.

Nobody challenged her. Everybody went back to what they were doing, including Concretia, who glared at Cinderella. She had murder in her eyes and a head of hair that was hazardous enough to pull it off, but she was going to have to file that chore away and put it on her to-do list for a later date.

I wished Cinderella had made the "anyone who wants to mess with the new girl has to come though me" speech before Concretia had conked me on the head, but I was glad she was on my side. Despite her being the one who got me into the situation in the first place, I liked Cinderella. It felt good to have a friend. And considering where I was, it felt even better to have a friend who appeared to have been born with the badass gene.

Cinderella and I sat down at one of the long tables in the cafeteria. On every side of the room, armed Sentries stood at attention, their eyes peeled for girl trouble. I don't know if they were expecting a riot, but considering the food in front of us, which was a slimy mixture of sludge, mush and gruel covered in raisins (at least I hope they were raisins), the only thing there could possibly be an outbreak of was food poisoning.

The other girls at the table avoided eye-contact with us. We were not welcome to sit and join them, and in normal circumstances, I would have complied and found a remote table to hide under, but Cinderella defiantly sat there anyway, and so did I (although not as defiantly).

But one of the girls, sitting right across from us, actually smiled at me.

She seemed tired but friendly, with thin strands of hair, like filthy angel hair pasta. Her back was straight, yet her face seemed hunched over.

"I have an extra apple," she said. "You can have it if you like."

That apple was the only edible thing I had seen since I entered the cafeteria. I was about to thank her, but then Cinderella frantically whispered to me, "No! Whatever you do…"

"Don't eat the apple?" I said. "Because it will cast some sort of poison spell on me?"

"Oh, go ahead and eat the apple," Cinderella said. "Just don't engage in conversation with her."

"But she seems nice."

She was nice. But I soon found out why Cinderella didn't want me to talk to her.

"Her name is Dronezzz," she said. "I should warn you about her."

To give you an idea of what Cinderella was warning me about, here is the Dronezzz storybook:

There was once a girl so vibrant and young
With a gift for gab and a sly tart tongue
Her conversation sparkled whenever she spoke
She was quick and clever and politically woke
But a backlash occurred, as might be expected
From insecure men who strongly objected
To the way she talked with intelligence and wit
So they decided to put an end to it
A spell was concocted that made everyone snore
Because it transformed her into a crashing bore
So instead of being charming, interesting and deep
Her conversation now puts people to sleep
So if you have insomnia, you can rest assured
That if you talk to Dronezzz you'll be instantly cured

I hadn't read her storybook when I met Dronezzz, and Cinderella didn't have time to explain all this to me, so I made the mistake of engaging her in conversation.

37

"Hi," I said. "I'm…"

But I never got the chance to say another word. She continued talking. And talking. And talking:

"You know, apples are one of the few things I'm allowed to eat because I'm on a vegan diet. That's right I'm a vegan. Did I mention I'm vegan? Are you familiar with the vegan lifestyle? Well, let me tell you step my step and item-by-item what I can and can't eat. Dairy is of course off limits, and that includes all forms of cheese. I eat vegetables, but only certain kinds, and never yellow ones. Oh, and I forgot to mention kale. The thing about kale is…"

Immediately after she began this monologue, I became drowsy, and as Dronezzz continued speaking, Cinderella whispered to me, "I tried to warn you. She is under a hundred-year spell where anyone she talks to is put to sleep by her conversation. Some of us have developed an immunity, but you…"

I wasn't immune, so somewhere between her filibuster about the importance of fiber and locally grown farm-to-table baked goods, I fell asleep.

This was a special kind of sleep. The minute I slipped into unconsciousness, I was back home. No one could see me, but I could view everything that was happening. I saw my father. I so wanted to talk to him, but I could only watch.

At first I thought I was dreaming, but I later found out that due to the nature of the spell Dronezzz was under, when she put you to sleep, you fell into a deep level of your subconscious that then transports you into a state of Astral Projection. So you silently and invisibly are able to fly to actual places in the conscious world. It was both wonderful and horrible. Wonderful because I could see my home and my dad. Horrible because I couldn't communicate with him. I could only hover and observe, which is what I did.

Dad was in the basement, looking around. Apparently he had returned from checking out mug shots at the police station and came home to find that I wasn't there.

"Laura? Laura, where are you?"

He was agitated. When he's in this state of mind, it usually means I'm in trouble, but in this case any trouble I might be in with my dad was way preferable to the trouble I was in with the awful characters running this reformatory.

"Damn it, Laura, where did you go? This is not like you!"

I so wanted to tell him that I was right there, but I couldn't, and he wasn't talking to me, he was talking to himself, as he often does. Dad is always muttering things for his own benefit. He spends a lot of time alone with his own thoughts because his brain is one of the few places where he feels welcome.

He passed by the wall where the trans-dimensional tunnel had been. But there was no mess or any sign that I had tunneled through the wall, and certainly no indication that I had broken down barriers that separate universes. For the first time in my life I was wishing that I was in trouble for not cleaning up after myself.

Dad stood still and just let his senses absorb everything for a moment. "Something happened here. I can feel it," he said.

That was dad's police detective instincts kicking in. They had served him well several times in the past, and had resulted in the arrest and conviction of many a perp (once his instincts were followed up with proper evidence and hard facts, that is).

In the process of burrowing into another word, I had caused no property damage, but I wished I had, because then Dad might have been able to find a clue about where to find me. But at this moment, he was perplexed and angry that he didn't know what in God's name was going on or where I was.

He moved his hand against the wall. "Come on, evidence," he said. "Reveal yourself to me."

I don't think Dad would like it if he knew that I knew he tried to talk evidence into presenting itself to him, but I fully understood that this was his process, what he had to go through to solve this case.

The trouble was, that sixth sense of his for solving crimes was useless because this was a crime that involved known associates of fictional characters from alternate realities. I mean, how would he even get a warrant for that?

It was frightening to think that my disappearance into a mysterious vortex might become a cold case that would last for all eternity.

My dad continued to investigate the wall, not quite knowing what he was looking for. And then, he pulled an iPad out of his back pocket. It was the tablet that Agent O had downloaded all my data to and then dropped on the lawn when Dad was trying to arrest him. Apparently Dad had found it in my bedroom and taken it down to the basement with him.

Dad held up the tablet and looked at the screen. I was certain that there was no way in hell that he knew my password. When your dad is a professional snoop, you do everything you can to protect whatever privacy you might have, so I made sure my password was something I had never said out loud or shared with the world; that's why I had complete confidence that no living human would ever figure out that all you had to do to break into my computer was type in "i heart gil davis".

But Dad was going to use his deductive reasoning to try to figure something out, so he started typing lord knows what into the keyboard, but the first key he hit, whatever it was, resulted in a a big spark of electricity shooting out of the tablet.

"The hell…?" he said.

Electrical currents began to dance before him, like a miniature lightning storm. I can tell you for a fact that I did not have any software on my computer that could possibly do something like this. This had to be something that had been originated on Agent O's iPad.

And sure enough, the electrical lightning flashes stopped, and when the smoke cleared, Agent O was standing in front of my dad. I guessed, and was later proven right, that Agent O had set his tablet so that someone, anyone, by hitting any random key, could retrieve him from the endless vortex of space and time if he happened to get trapped there. This was a good app to have, and I'd recommend it to anyone who frequently travels between cosmic dimensions.

But Dad, considering Agent O to be a dangerous criminal who was quite possibly involved with the disappearance of his daughter, did something unprofessional. He punched Agent O hard across his face. I could see from Dad's expression that this was an impulsive act he was was never going to regret for the rest of his life. The big Ogre fell backwards and hit the wall, puncturing the plaster and blasting apart several bricks. The force of Dad's punch did what a trans-dimensional wormhole had failed to do: it caused a mess on our basement floor.

Dad grabbed Agent O by his lapel and threw him back against the wall, causing even more damage.

"Where is my daughter!" he demanded. "And how the hell did you just suddenly appear in my basement out of nowhere?"

It was a good question, and I was looking forward to hearing the answer.

But then I woke up.

My slumber had ended because Dronezzz had moved down the table and was putting another girl to sleep with her conversation.

I turned to Cinderella and said, "The sleep-state that Dronezzz put me under enabled me to see my dad back at my house. Agent O has emerged from the trans-dimensional netherworld and Dad has made contact with him."

"Did you see what he was doing?"

"Yeah, he was in the process of arresting Agent O."

"We've got to get in touch with Agent FG before anything else happens," Cinderella said. "Otherwise, we may never get out of here."

I felt like throwing up. But there wasn't any prison food in my stomach to hurl because I hadn't eaten anything. Skipping dinner in this horrid place was one of the few wise decisions I had recently made.

CHAPTER SEVEN

"How are we going to get in touch with Agent FG?" I asked, as Cinderella and I took our trays of mostly uneaten "food" and threw them in the recycling bin (I didn't want to think about where that recycling ended up. Back for a return engagement on our plates was my nauseating guess).

"Agent FG will get in touch," Cinderella said. "But we have to do certain things to make sure she knows we want her to contact us. Here's what we've got to do…"

She didn't say anything more because at that moment Dr. Strepgoat appeared at a podium on a stage on the other side of the room facing the tables. He said, "Hear ye, hear ye!"

Everybody pretty much ignored him, so he yelled, "I said, *HEAR YE, HEAR YE, BITCHES!*"

This got everyone's attention. We all turned and faced him to hear ye hear ye what he had to say.

"I have a very important announcement to make," he said.

He paused dramatically, and then announced, "The Prince is coming."

This news was greeted with more awkward silence.

Finally, somebody asked, "Where? Where is he coming?"

"To this institution!" Dr. Strepgoat said. "To this very cafeteria."

Now he got the reaction he was going for. A general murmur of excitement went up among all the gals.

"He wants to show his subjects in the Fairy Tale Commonwealth that he cares about you pathetic turds," he said. "After all that unpleasantness with

Cinderella, he seeks to reestablish himself as the favorite of all fair maidens throughout the land, even you losers."

I was starting to figure out that Dr. Strepgoat believed the key to rehabilitation for a young female delinquent was constant berating and belittling, so I knew I needed to be careful because I still had just enough self-esteem to be considered a danger to the status quo.

"It's going to be a special brunch held right here," he said. Then his eyes widened as he added, "And here's an additional delightful piece of news. Cinderella is not invited."

Everyone turned and looked at Cinderella with sneering smiles, but Cinderella just sneered and smiled right back at them. If she cared at all about what the Prince thought of her, she certainly wasn't showing it.

"Everyone here who qualifies and passes our screening process will have elegant ball gowns magically bestowed upon them," Strepgoat said. "It will be a formal affair, so I cannot have you looking like the filthy, disgusting unholy trash you really are."

I guess his attitude was: if you can't say something nice about someone, say it over and over again. But that didn't matter, because everyone in the room was becoming increasingly more excited. The idea of looking good and being decked out like a princess held a genuine appeal, even to a bunch of filthy, disgusting unholy trash like us.

And I have to admit I was a bit excited myself. I believed Cinderella when she told me the Prince was an evil fascist dictator and all, but still, based on the pictures of him I had seen hung up everywhere in this institution, he was pretty darn cute, you know, as far as evil fascist dictators go.

But in my defense, all of this was hypothetical. It wasn't a surefire thing that I would even get to meet the Prince, and if I did meet him, I was supposed to assassinate him, which I'm sure would have made a second date highly unlikely.

"Everyone will undergo a review and an evaluation to determine if you are emotionally ready to be in the same room with the Prince," Dr. Strepgoat said. "Some of you are already disqualified, and by some of you, I mean, Cinderella."

Cinderella laughed the kind of laugh that is hostile to the very idea of laughing, while the thought of her being banned from the brunch brought out a feeling of glee from the other girls. They had no reason to dislike her, but they did, because resentment was one of the few extracurricular activities allowed in this place.

Amid all the noisy chatter about the Prince's brunch, Cinderella whispered to me, "This could work in our favor. The fact that the Prince is coming here could give us the perfect opportunity to kill him once and for all."

To be honest, this wasn't what I was interested in hearing at that moment. I mean, come on, I'm sixteen, which is perhaps a bit too old to be getting caught up in the excitement of meeting a handsome Prince, but also maybe kind of young to be getting involved in a conspiracy to violently overthrow a repressive regime. I had become a "tween" in the worst possible way.

When Cinderella had leaned in and whispered to me, I could see Dr. Strepgoat staring directly at us. I knew that I was already linked with Cinderella in everybody's mind, especially Dr. Strepgoat, and this meant that I was almost certainly not going to qualify for attendance at the Prince's brunch.

This was good in a way, I guess, because if I wasn't going to attend the Prince's Brunch, that meant I wasn't going to be in any position to kill him, and that was fine with me.

But despite her trying to involve me in a bloody coup, and even though I'd only known her for a short time, I liked Cinderella and I valued her friendship. Was this a sad commentary on my overall social incompetence in this or any other dimension? Of course it was, but I thought Cinderella was cool and I loved that she liked me.

But now the opportunity of going to the Prince's Brunch and meet him was turning my brain into a smoothy blender of opposing thoughts.

There was a part of me that felt if I met the Prince, I could maybe change him and transform him into a good person and then perhaps we could become boyfriend and girlfriend and eventually marry and then live an endlessly joyful life with no problems or any unhappiness ever.

But I didn't want to assassinate him because that just seemed unrealistic.

CHAPTER EIGHT

As we were leaving the cafeteria, Cinderella said, "Believe me, the Prince is nothing to get excited about. He's the biggest bore in the world. And ball gowns are overrated. They're scratchy and uncomfortable. They weigh a ton, and if you try to do anything in them but bow and curtsey, you'll spend the rest of your life going to a chiropractor."

"I'm sure it's better than wearing a straitjacket," I said.

"It's no different from a straitjacket," Cinderella replied. "It's meant to have the same effect: to confine you, except instead of buckles and straps, the restraint is conformity. The only advantage of a ball gown over a straitjacket is that you can scratch your nose, but a so-called 'proper lady' is not supposed to scratch her nose anyway, so there's really no difference."

I didn't doubt that her words were true. Still, I so wanted to wear one of those sparkly dresses. I guess I had never outgrown the princess phase I went through when I was a little girl. I was still into it, except when I was a kid it was cute and cuddly, now it felt more like a masochistic 50 Shades of Gown kind of thing.

We were almost out of the room when we saw Dr. Strepgoat coming towards us.

"What does he want now?" Cinderella said.

But it was a surprise to both of us when Strepgoat said, "Laura, I want to speak with you."

"I'll try to get in touch with Agent FG," Cinderella whispered. "Have fun talking to Strepgoat."

Cinderella walked away, leaving me alone to face my half-man/half-goat/all-idiot jailer.

Strepgoat looked at me and shook his head sadly, as if observing an accident that could have been prevented.

"You've become very friendly with Cinderella, haven't you?" he said.

"We hang out," was all I could think to say.

"Well, young lady, if you want to keep getting into trouble, then continue commiserating with Cinderella."

"She's the only one in this place who's been nice to me," I said.

It's weird. I was trying to justify my friendship with Cinderella to him, which is something I shouldn't have had to do, because, really, when you come right down to it, who gives a damn what he thinks of me and who I hang out with? But I was also aware that he did have a point – my friendship with Cinderella, who was a revolutionary and a firebrand, was going to get me into more trouble. From what I've learned in history class, people who become involved in overthrows of authoritarian governments often live romantic, heroic lives. In other words, they die young.

But Cinderella was the only person in the entire reform school who seemed to care about what happened to me. But I also knew that her efforts to help me might ultimately hurt me.

All of these conflicting thoughts were making my head hurt, so I said the only thing that seemed appropriate:

"Do you have any aspirin?"

"You listen to me, young lady," he said. "You're going to need a lot more than aspirin if you don't straighten up and fly right, missy."

Oh, great. He had used both "young lady" and "missy." Things just kept getting worse and worse. And as he walked away, it was quite clear that he wasn't going to give me any aspirin.

I went in the opposite direction and it wasn't long before I found Cinderella waiting for me.

"Good news," she said. "I've just been told that I have a visitor. It must be Agent FG! Maybe she's received some sort of communiqué about Agent O. This could be my ticket out of here and your ticket back home!"

I wanted to cry with joy, but I knew that joy was against the law in this place, so instead I kept my up mood on the down low and just hugged Cinderella. My sudden impulse to openly express emotion made me think that whatever part of the fairy tale kingdom I was in, it probably wasn't the midwestern part.

"Well, well, well," I heard a voice say. Of course it was Dr. Strepgoat again, standing in the hallway and taking in our embrace with a look of epic disapproval.

It didn't surprise me that in addition to "young lady" and "missy," he also used "well, well, well" in his repertoire of stupid phrases that jerky adults say.

"You just don't know how to take good advice, do you?" Strepgoat said.

"What's your point?" Cinderella replied, unaware that he was talking to me, not her.

"Please, Cinderella," he said. "Continue on. I don't want to prevent you from seeing your visitors."

"Visitors?" Cinderella said. This was her first indication that maybe it wasn't her Fairy Godmother who was there to see her.

"Yes," Strepgoat replied. "Your stepmother and stepsisters."

"Oh, for God's sake, spare me," Cinderella said, turning away from him. "Tell them to get lost."

"You are obligated to visit with them," Strepgoat said.

"Since when is that a rule?"

"Since I made it a rule, just now."

"Well, I refuse to go."

"Okay, you can have a choice. You can visit your lovely step-siblings, who were nice enough to go through the trouble of coming to visit. Or, you can sit in a padded cell for the next month, straitjacketed and gagged. Your choice."

"A month?" Cinderella said dismissively. "I can do that time standing on my head."

Cinderella's willingness to say something so defiant at such a moment was one of the things I most admired about her. It was so the opposite of my personality.

"Don't mess with me, young lady," Strepgoat said. "What's it going to be?"

Cinderella stood in angry silence.

"Well?" Strepgoat said.

"Okay, okay," Cinderella said. "I'll have a nice visit with the Evils."

"They're your flesh and blood!" Strepgoat said.

"They are not my flesh and blood! I have no flesh and blood left in this world!"

There was a crack in Cinderella's voice as she said this, a vulnerable sound, as if something deep within her was gasping for air. I knew that sound. It was a wavering noise, like your vocal cords have tripped over something and are trying not to fall. It's the kind of crack that had appeared in my voice many times after my mother died.

Strepgoat responded with his usual compassion. "Whatever," he said. "Just get over to the visitors room right now."

Cinderella started to go, and Strepgoat said to me, "And you'd better heed what I said, missy. You'd best keep your distance from Cinderella. She is not like you at all."

This prompted me to impulsively say, "I'm going with Cinderella. I want to meet her step-sibbies."

Cinderella turned and gave me a quizzical look.

"They're famous villains," I said. "Celebrities. Maybe I can get their autograph."

Cinderella smiled. She knew I was kidding, that I was really just coming along for moral support.

But of course Strepgoat didn't get it because he doesn't get anything.

"Do whatever you want," he sighed, throwing up his hooves. "It's your funeral."

Cinderella and I walked past Strepgoat and towards the visitor's room. I was happy to be showing solidarity with Cinderella, but I was worried. Very worried. Because I knew that what Strepgoat just said was no idle threat.

Gruesome deaths happen in fairy tales almost as often as they happen in horror fiction.

So, yeah, it might very well be my funeral.

CHAPTER NINE

Just as we were about to reach the visitor's room, Cinderella turned to me and said, "Are you sure you're ready for this?"

"Yeah, I guess," I said.

"Good, because I'm not."

A Sentry opened the door and we entered the visitor's room.

Three women, heavily de-beautified by beauty products, sat at the visitor's table.

They were not exactly what I expected.

I immediately knew that the oldest of the three, the one with the severe face tightened by witchcraft-enhanced cosmetic surgery, was the stepmom.

The two stepsisters, not much older than Cinderella, sat on either side of their mother. I have to say, it was a chore to look at them. They had classic fair maiden features, the kind of bland beauty that fashion magazine editors base their philosophy of life on, but their faces were contorted from constant pain; not surprising, considering that parts of both their pairs of feet had recently been severed after they decapitated them in an attempt to fit into that glass slipper.

You've heard the expression – it was horrifying, but I couldn't look away? Well, this wasn't like that at all. It was easy to look away. Very easy.

The stepmother pointed at me. "Who the hell is this?" she said.

"A friend," Cinderella replied, as we both sat down on the opposite side of the table.

"She must be a loser if she's a friend of yours, Cinderella," the stepsister to her right said.

This was Lanolin, the older of the two. Her voice sounded like a tractor plowing a sidewalk.

"Please don't say anything you might regret," Cinderella said. "You don't want to put your foot in your mouth. Oh, wait, you don't have a foot."

I laughed. Just the small, shy kind of laugh that I usually make, but Lanolin screamed at me, "You bitch! I worked really hard cutting and mutilating myself to win the Prince's love. How dare you mock me for being a romantic."

"My sister's self-inflicted wounds are not her fault!" the other stepsister said.

This was Liceeta, a bit younger than Lanolin, but no less unpleasant. Her voice was similar to her sister's, but louder and higher-pitched, on a frequency only dogs and everyone else can hear.

One thing was certain: these gals did not like Cinderella, and they treated her like dirt. This part of the storybook legend was true. For centuries, these ladies and other characters in various books and movies had given step-relatives a bad name. This is not cool, because a lot of kids at my school have step-mothers or step-fathers or step-brothers or step-sisters, and it all seems normal and from what I can see they're not any better or any worse than anyone else.

My point is that the stereotype of the evil stepmother is a harmful cliche.

Anyway, Cinderella's evil stepmother leaned forward and said, "We came here to tell you something." A smile began to form on her lips, the kind of forced smile that seems like it's been read off a karaoke machine. "I have made a generous contribution to this reformatory in your father's name."

"Oh?" Cinderella said. "You've found a new way to piss all over his memory. Cool!"

"That's just the sort of smart mouth that got you where you are," the stepmother continued. "And that is why I am helping the administration open a new Lobotomy Wing. The wizards, alchemists and sorcerers in the Prince's employ are working on a new brain-modification device that will extract the individuality of all sassy young malcontent maidens like yourself and turn every one of you into compliant courtesans no longer constrained by the burden of personality. What do you think about that?"

"Big deal," Cinderella said, in the indifferent tone of a Marvel fanatic being told about a new DC movie. But I could see fear in her eyes. Nobody, no matter how cutting edge, wants the edge of their frontal lobe cut off.

"We just wanted you to know that your days of being able to talk without a drool bucket are numbered," Lanolin said.

"I'm just glad I can contribute, if even for just a little bit, to the good of our society," the stepmother added. "Once I see you eating paste and babbling like a village idiot, I'll know that I have changed the world for the better."

"You three are already lobotomized," Cinderella said, addressing them like a hostile witness at a Senate committee hearing. "You've been that way since you were little girls and became willing subjects of a totalitarian regime that forbids individual freedom. But I'm still my father and my mother's daughter — my real mother's daughter — and I always will be. She may be gone, but she taught me to think independently and to be true to myself. There's nothing you can do to change that."

"Actually," Liceeta said. "We can change that. By removing a large part of your brain, we can dull your senses to the point where they won't exist. Yup, pretty much, we can do that."

Although we hated to admit it to ourselves, what she was saying was hypothetically true. If you can't destroy a person's spirit by constantly insulting them and doing everything in your power to make them feel like a lower species of human being, you can just go inside their heads and do it physically, if you have the resources. And they did have the money and the power and thus the resources, so this was scary.

Then, just to make conversation I guess, the stepmother turned to me and said, "You should be ashamed of yourself for being friends with Cinderella. You're a disgrace to your father and mother."

"Leave my parents out of this," I said in a calm, measured voice. "My mother is dead and you have no right to talk about her."

"Of course!" Lanolin said, waving her jangly, QVC-encrusted hand at me. "Another member of the dead mommy club. Too bad you don't have older stepsisters to whip you into shape."

I didn't want to stoop to her level.

"Shut up, bitch," I said.

Yeah, I stooped to her level. It felt great.

It's odd, but even though the stepmother mentioning my mom was what got me all riled up, it was my dad whose spirit I was channeling. I wanted to line these sad pathetic excuses up against a wall, cuff them, read them their rights, and throw their asses in jail. But what sucked was that I was the one whose ass was in jail.

Cinderella put her hand on my shoulder. "They're not worth the bother," she said. "Just hang loose and wait for one of them to try to get the Prince to notice them. Then they'll cut off another limb. When it comes to hurting them, they don't need outside contractors. They do it all themselves."

Sentries were summoned and we were escorted out of the room. Cinderella's step-sibs had declared the meeting over. They had let Cinderella know that they were planning on having her turned into a vegetable, so as far as the purpose of their visit was concerned, it was Mission Accomplished.

As we were walking away from the visitor's room, Cinderella turned to me and said. "I don't know if you noticed, but I don't really get along with my relatives."

We both laughed. I had heard about this sort of thing. It was called bonding. Cinderella and I had a kinship. We were both in the dead mommy club. We were both in the only child club. And we were both in the soon-to-be-lobotomized club, which was terrifying.

Still, it was nice to have a sense of belonging.

CHAPTER TEN

We returned to the main area of the reformatory. The impending Prince's Brunch had inspired a feeling of giddiness among all the other girls. Everyone was excited by the idea of their humdrum, desperate, hopeless lives becoming slightly less humdrum, desperate, and hopeless for an hour or so.

Cinderella and I passed Concretia, who was sitting with her posse, a bunch of girls that where so pasty and glum, they managed, without costuming or makeup, to look like goth vampires, achieving this effect solely on the basis of their own despair.

Concretia was talking loudly, because she wanted Cinderella to hear every word she said.

"This visit from the Prince is our chance to rewrite history," she announced. "Cinderella soured the Prince on fair maidens, but this is the prefect opportunity for us to show him that we're not all losers like Cinderella."

Everyone at Concretia's table knew that Cinderella could hear her and although I think it was painful for them to crane their necks, they all looked over at us to see how she would react.

But Cinderella ignored them, or, perhaps, pretended to ignore them. As we walked away from them, I turned to Cinderella and said, "I'm guessing the storybook I read and gave a four star recommendation for didn't tell the whole story, so please tell me what really happened when you went to the Prince's Ball."

She seemed reluctant to talk about her past, but she filled me in as we continued walking: "Well, regardless of which Cinderella story you read, there's always the part where my mom dies, and then my dad remarries and hooks up with an evil stepmother who brings along her two equally evil stepdaughters, and then my dad dies and now my stepmom is my legal guardian and she and her daughters treat me like garbage, but then a fairy godmother comes along and whips me up a fancy ball gown and I go to the Prince's ball and then everything is all happily-whatever-after, you know that story, right?"

"Of course."

"Well, a lot of it is true, but the happily-ever-after part was made up by some hack writer who threw in an upbeat ending just to increase book sales."

"Yeah, the happily-ever-after thing is very commercial. I'm sure it helped sell books."

"I know, but I changed the story. I'll admit, I was a filthy wench under the thumb of an awful stepmom and stepsisters. I was forced to cook and clean and wait on them like some kind of domestic servant with no minimum wage salary or benefits or collective bargaining rights. But then the Prince's Ball happened, blah, blah, blah, and my Fairy Godmother turned a pumpkin into a blah, blah, blah, and I go to the ball and the Prince asks me to dance like a million times, and…"

"Blah, blah, blah?" I said, trying to be helpful.

"Actually, no!" Cinderella said. "I won't dismiss that part of the story with any blah, blah, blah, because in truth it was great. The Prince was into me, and it was the total opposite of my regular life and I was having a great time."

"Then, the clocked struck Midnight, and…"

"Listen, the 'clock struck midnight' thing is way overblown. My understanding was that I had use of the carriage all night, and I didn't have to return the dress until the next morning. I think the powers-that-be decided that the third act needed to be punched up and the stakes had to be raised, or some crap like that."

"Well," I said. "It's the romantic part of the story that I was always into. And you liked the Prince at first, right?"

"At first? Totally! Who wouldn't? He was good-looking, and he could dance."

"Sounds awesome."

"It was. The only thing that put a damper on the evening was when he did that one annoying thing."

"What's that?"

"He started talking. Oh, my God! What a bore! He chattered on and on and on about his favorite topic — himself. He had no interest in me, or anything about my life, and it quickly became apparent that he saw me as nothing more than an ornamental addition to his wardrobe. But up to that point it was a fun evening, a real morale booster. I was ready to go home and shove my belle-of-the-ball-ness in my stepsister's faces and prepare to live my life differently. The thing is, even though it was clear that I didn't have any chemistry with the Prince, the whole evening was still amazing because it inspired me to pursue a better life. I vowed from that moment forward to pick myself up and get the hell out of my house and do something, you know, find some meaning, pursue a career, become someone. I wasn't going to live my life based on a pre-exiting story that had already been written about me without my knowledge or input."

"But what was your fairy godmother's reason for turning you into the belle of the ball?"

"Well, she later told me that part of what she does as a secret agent is disguise herself as a whimsical fairy so she can recruit people like me to help take down the monarchy. She was hoping that I'd go home with the Prince and win his confidence, and then at the right moment, murder him in his sleep."

"You know, I hate to say this, but there is something passive-aggressive about your Fairy Godmother."

"I know. But I ultimately screwed up her plan as well. Apparently, I can't please anybody."

"But at the end of that night, weren't you disappointed that you didn't at least get a boyfriend out of the whole deal?"

"Oh, I was hoping to meet my soulmate that night. But in order for someone to be a soulmate, they have to have a soul, so the Prince didn't qualify.

"What a drag. If you can't meet the guy of your dreams in a fairy tale, where are you going to meet him?"

"I'm not sure, but I believe he's out there somewhere. However, that's a moot point because I'm not going to be a part of any kind of dating scene as long as I'm locked up in this reformatory."

"I have to admit I am sorry it didn't work out with you and the Prince."

"Look, I would have been willing to date him a few more times, and even make-out with him, but I didn't want it to go further than that because if I had lived happily ever after with him I would have been miserable. When I broke up with him and said I wanted to see other people, that's when everyone decided I was crazy and they threw me in here."

"That is such a sad story."

"Well, you wanted to hear it."

"To be honest, if I were a writer of fairy tale storybooks, I would have embellished and changed the ending just like the other writers did. And you may not be willing to admit it, but the stroke-of-midnight device is a great plot point, it adds suspense, and totally drives the story into the third act."

"Sounds to me like maybe you should be a writer," Cinderella said.

As an aspiring writer, it meant a lot to hear her say this. To have a fictional character tell you that you should write fiction is validating as all get-out.

"Yeah, I have thought about being a writer," I admitted, saying it out loud for the first time. "And I have to be honest, the ending of the story you just told is not particularly satisfying."

"I know. That's why I'm trying to change it."

A Sentry approached us and told Cinderella to report to the infirmary.

"What for?"

"Routine cooties inspection."

That didn't sound like an actual thing, but the Sentry was carrying a large weapon, so Cinderella had no choice but to comply.

The Sentry then turned to me and said, "You have to report to a Prince's Brunch orientation meeting."

Cinderella and I exchanged a look. It was unspoken but we knew that every time we were separated, it could be the last time we'd ever see each other.

And there was an even bigger possibility that when the storybooks of our lives were ultimately written, the endings of our stories might be even more depressing than the one she just told me.

CHAPTER ELEVEN

I arrived in an assembly room where several other girls were already seated in rusty folding chairs that were uncomfortable to even look at. I sat down just as one of the reform school's supervisory witches stepped up to a podium to address us.

She was a woman with eyes that had all the radiance of a steel mill. She might have been attractive once. She might still be attractive. But she had been led to believe otherwise, so loneliness had settled like cold cream on her face.

"Okay, listen up, Girly-Qs," she said, holding up a long dark stick. "This is a magic wand. You've all seen them, and some of you have used them, and most of you have abused them. But if you are approved to attend the Prince's Brunch, a magic wand will be waved at you for the first time since you've been incarcerated."

She shifted her position slightly and this was the first time any of us realized a small unsteady girl was standing next to her. I don't want to say she appeared under-the-weather, but she looked like the kind of person the word gesundheit was invented for.

"This is Thumbelina," the matron said.

Wow, Thumbelina! She was the only iconic storybook celebrity I had seen here besides Cinderella. She was taller and bigger than I thought she'd be. She'd qualify as carry-on, but I doubt if you could fit her underneath the seat in front of you. Her most striking feature was not her size but her sizable health issues. She should have called-in sick but I'm sure that wasn't an option.

Thumbelina coughed. She appeared malnourished, which was not a shock, considering the quality of the reformatory food. And she seemed desperately unhappy, which was even less of a shock, considering the quality of everything here.

But then the Witch waved the wand and Thumbelina's wrinkly orange jump suit was magically replaced by a sparkly ball gown, and all at once her complexion appeared to be that of an elite prep school girl just back from a Caribbean vacation.

The expression on her face changed not a bit. This transformation she experienced was purely cosmetic and not the least bit emotional. The magic wand did not make her one bit happier, yet that didn't stop most of the girls in the room from gasping, cheering, and applauding. Considering the conditions we were living under, I guess I couldn't blame them for being easily entertained.

The general tone of everyone seemed to be: how enchanting that you are now a better dressed miserable person than you were two seconds ago. Ooh! Ah!

But I'd be lying if I said I wasn't also impressed with Thumbelina's new look. I'd like to think that I am above these sorts of things, but I'm not. I've always wished I had a fashion sense that turned heads as I entered a room. But my sense of "style" has always had the opposite effect. No matter what I wear to school, I am always dressed in the same garment — a cloak of invisibility. There is only one instance of me turning heads when I entered a room and that was this one time when I walked into my high school cafeteria and bumped into a cart of plates and silverware and loudly knocked it all to the floor. Yes, heads turned, but this was immediately followed by the word "dork" ricocheting from table to table.

I remember it well because it's the only time Gil Davis ever noticed me. And the reason I had knocked into the cart was because I was staring at him while he stared into space. When I caused the commotion, he looked away from whatever far-away abstraction he was contemplating and glanced at me for a single moment and then went back to staring into the dark nothingness of the abyss, which was apparently more interesting than looking at me. It was the closest we had ever come to having an interaction and I have to say it was less than satisfying.

Anyway, the Witch waved the wand a second time, and Thumbelina was now once again a sickly girl in an orange jumpsuit. Her expression changed not at all. The Witch gave her the nod to leave, and she turned and walked away, a simple act that took a great deal of effort on her part.

"A complete evaluation will be given of every girl in the reformatory," the Witch continued. "It is a rare privilege to be in the presence of the Prince. He doesn't allow just anyone to look at him, and he is meticulous and selective about who he will consent to look at. The fact that he is coming here and is willing to allow you to even be in the same room with him is an act of generosity unparalleled in the history of all existence. You are not worthy of him and yet he is actually going to give you the time of day. What a great man! I'll tell you one thing, I wish I was in a relationship. But, alas, my desires are restricted by the rules of this regime. I am not allowed to freely choose a mate. So I have nothing. *NOTHING!*"

Everyone was startled by her sudden intensity. Out of the blue, she had pulled open the storm window to her soul, and now there was no holding her back.

"Why shouldn't I have someone in my life? Why am I not allowed to have dreams?" she asked of no one and everyone. "Why do I have to be alone? I deserve as much a shot at happiness as anyone! When it comes to loving and being loved, why not me? Why not me?"

And with that, she waved the wand over her own body and was immediately transformed from super-witch to super-model. Her hair was blonde, her face was smooth, and the manufactured perfection of her new body was apparent to all since she was wearing only a bikini. If an advertising executive had been around, he would have instantly given her a beer product to sell during a Super Bowl commercial.

"I'm the new princess!" she screamed. "I'm the new princess!"

By now an alarm had gone off, which it turns out is what happens anytime anyone in the reformatory engages in unauthorized magic, or, even more egregious, unauthorized yearning.

Dr. Strepgoat, along with several Sentries, burst into the room.

"Seize her!" Strepgoat commanded, and the Sentries all rushed to the podium and grabbed her while she continued to flail about and scream at the top of her lungs, "I want love! I want love! I want love!"

I want love. No kidding. She was just saying what everybody is always thinking, poor thing.

I was horrified, not by the spectacle of a freak-out, but by the nightmare of a person revealing something natural and basic about herself in such a public setting. I am always afraid of being exposed, of being found out, of people discovering what I want and how I'm feeling. At school I am always afraid that if I reveal who I really am, no one will like me. So even when I'm walking out in the open, down the school hallway between classes, I'm trying to stay hidden. It's not that I want to be alone; I desperately want social acceptance. I wish people knew the real me, the true me, the person I actually am. And when they finally get to know that person, I hope they'll introduce me to her because I have idea who the hell that is.

I just want people to like me for who I wish I was.

Anyway, the Sentries got the situation under control. The wand was waved and the Witch's career as a bikini model was over before it even started; her body was once again completely covered with her drab matronly prison uniform, although her emotional nakedness continued to linger.

Dr. Strepgoat then clip-clopped up to the podium and announced, "Pay no attention to what you have just seen. The Prince's Brunch will continue as planned. You will be called in for your evaluation in a random order that I will chose based solely on favoritism. Sign the sheet, then get out of my sight!"

There was much pushing and shoving as everyone raced to get on line to sign up. I lackadaisically meandered to the back of the line. Anyone looking at me would think that meeting the Prince didn't matter much, and if Cinderella had been there, that's what I would have wanted her to think.

But the truth was, I did want to meet the Prince. I didn't want to want to meet him, but I did want to meet him. God help me.

As I stood in line, Strepgoat approached me.

"After you've signed the sheet, I want you to come into my office," he said. "I need to speak with you about something."

Oh, crap. Now what?

CHAPTER TWELVE

Being summoned by Dr. Strepgoat was terrifying, because I'm not the kind of girl that ever even gets sent to the principal's office. I behave myself. I study and do my homework. I keep my head low and stay out of trouble. Yup, I'm that boring.

Not drawing attention to myself has always come naturally to me. Sure, every now and then Mean Girls bully me at school about my nerdy geekiness or my geeky nerdiness, but that's just a mundane circumstance for anyone who crosses the geek/nerd threshold as often as I do.

But I don't usually get into trouble with authority figures. Of course I never want my dad to be mad at me, although it might surprise some people to know that he is not a screamer, at least when it comes to his daughter. When he's angry with me, he usually just glares and retreats into a stoic silence that is worse than the loudest angry outburst. There is no more upsetting noise than the sound of my dad's silence when he's pissed off.

Dr. Strepgoat is probably the scariest authority figure I've ever encountered, and I find that a bit odd. He isn't tall or imposing, and the bottom half of his body looks no different from a farm animal that goes to the bathroom wherever it happens to be standing. I shouldn't be intimidated. I should just be grossed out.

But since I was locked up in this otherworldly institution with no rights, he had a power over me that my school Principal, with his vague, mild threats about no roughhousing in hallway, just didn't have.

My point is that getting called into Dr. Strepgoat's office all by myself was the type of thing I had spent my whole life trying to avoid. Earlier, when I was in his office, it was less scary because I was with Cinderella. But now I was flying solo as a newbie juvey.

"Sit down," Strepgoat said, in a surprisingly unthreatening tone. He pointed to a lounging area with a couple of plush swivel chairs.

I did as I was told. I sat down. He sat opposite me. Good lord, it was disturbing to see a half-man/half-goat make himself comfortable and cross his legs. Deeply disturbing.

I was so scared that inside my head I kept repeating to myself – be brave, be brave, be brave, be brave…

"I don't know much about you," Dr. Strepgoat said, scratching his left hoof with his right hoof. "You're a bit of a mystery."

Be brave, be brave, be brave, be brave…

"I only know that you're an accomplice of Cinderella and that you tried to help her escape. Do you realize how dire the consequences of this action are?"

Be brave, be brave, be… I began sobbing, the whole "be brave" thing burning like a daily affirmation written on flash paper.

"I just want to go home," I cried. "Please let me go home."

"I've learned about the earthly realm from whence you came," he said, handing me a box of tissues. "Much has been written about us fairy tale citizens in your world, but your media focuses on the sensationalistic aspects of the enchanted world, and glorifies our more disreputable characters – the Hansel and Gretels, the Sleeping Beauties, the Snow Whites, the Red Robin Hoods, the Goldilockses, and yes, the Cinderellas — they're the ones who get all the attention at the expense of the more worthwhile citizens of the storybook world, like for instance, yours truly."

Wow. What an ego on this guy. But maybe I could get his ego to work on my behalf. At least that was my thinking at the moment.

"Please, sir," I said. "I'm not part of the earthly realm media. I would love to read a storybook about you, really I would. I mean, you're a doctor and a successful government official. I think it would be so enlightening and educational if kids in my school read stories about you."

I assumed he would see right though my sucking up to him, but his ego was such that he bought into what I was saying.

"You are so right about that!" he said, perking up. "But unfortunately, being part of a best selling storybook in your world is so political, it's all about who you know. It makes me so angry!"

Uh oh. Now his mood was darkening again. Maybe I had miscalculated.

"And I also know that there are subversive elements in this world that are trying to recruit people from your world into a plot to overthrow the Prince and stage a fairy tale coup."

"I wouldn't know anything about that!" I said, lying through my chattering teeth.

"Really? Well, I received a negative report about you from Cinderella's stepmother and stepsisters. They believe that you should be lobotomized, along with Cinderella."

This was the scariest thing I had heard so far. The threat of having my brain removed was more than I could handle. I'm quite fond of my brain, it's always been the one thing in life I could count on, even if it was the main source of my thorough nerdification.

I fell apart.

"Please don't lobotomize me," I cried. "You don't know me, I'm a good girl, really, I am! Please, please, please, don't turn me into a drooling vegetable!"

I don't know how much of this was intelligible because I was sobbing so hard I sounded like I was underwater.

"Do you renounce Cinderella and all her evil Cinderella-ness?" Strepgoat said.

"Yes!" I replied without hesitation.

Of course, I didn't really want to renounce any of Cinderella's so-called evil Cinderella-ness, but I wanted to go home, and I sure didn't want to be instantly lobotomized. The slow, gradual lobotomization that comes from constant exposure to America's consumerist culture was much more my speed.

The tears were pouring down my cheeks like a windshield in a hurricane. "I only met Cinderella earlier today," I blubbered. "I had the wrong impression of her. I thought she was the ultimate fairy tale happily-ever-after fair maiden. I didn't know she was La Femme Nikita."

There was some truth to what I was saying. I honestly didn't know Cinderella until earlier that day. And I did have the wrong impression of her. The only little detail I left out was that I had always thought of her as a princess, but now I realized she was a warrior princess, and I loved that about her. I thought she was cool. But I sure wasn't going to say that to him.

Strepgoat cracked a smile that was meant to be benevolent, but came off as next-level creepy.

"You seem contrite and willing to sublimate your personality," he said "That is encouraging. I think the Prince will like you. Congratulations. You have been approved to attend the Prince's brunch."

"And then can I go home?"

"That will completely depend on your behavior."

"Do you even have the ability to send me back to my home in my own dimension?" I asked.

"That will not be a problem. Trans-dimensional travel can be arranged if you have access to the right kind of magic, which of course I do. What's important is that you be a good girl, and even more importantly, that you stop spending so much time with Cinderella. Do you think you can do that?"

"Yes sir," I said in my most submissive tone. I was winning the Olympic Gold Medal in ass-kissing. I'd like to think that I was playing him, but I was just being a huge wuss.

He gave me some more tissues, patted me on my head, and sent me on my way. God, how I hated him.

But I hated myself even more.

CHAPTER THIRTEEN

Cinderella was waiting for me soon after I left Dr. Strepgoat's office.

"Come here," she said. "I've got something to show you."

She grabbed my arm and pulled me along so quickly, I didn't have time to make up an excuse to not hang out with her. I needed a moment to figure out a way to make it seem like I wasn't blowing her off, although that's exactly what I was intending to do.

"I bet you want to know how my cooties inspection went," she said. I thought she was being sarcastic, but then she added, "It was great! I didn't have cooties when I got there, but within no time I was crawling with them."

"Oh?" I said, hoping to end the conversation. I really didn't want to talk about cooties.

"Agent FG arranged the whole thing. She cast a spell that surrounded me with a wall of cooties. But they were good cooties."

"Good cooties?"

"Yeah, cooties get a bad rap, but these magical ones created a barrier between me and the rest of the world. Agent FG and I were able to talk without the Sentries being able to see or hear us. So now the coast is clear for you to come along and meet with Agent FG as well."

There was a conspiratorial tone in Cinderella's voice, along with an air of menace. Exactly what I didn't need. I was once again publicly hanging around with Cinderella for everyone to see. And this was happening immediately after I promised the hoofed dingus who controls my fate that I would stop associating with her. And what's worse, now Cinderella was dragging me along to meet with a covert secret agent who was trying to bring down the fairy tale monarchy, and this meeting could very well lead to me being lobotomized.

But then I noticed something weird. Everybody else in the reformatory was ignoring us. It was as if Cinderella and I weren't there.

"We're invisible," she explained. "The cooties that Agent FG infected me with just made me invisible, and now I've infected you with that cootie. We'd better hurry, it only lasts for a short period of time."

I did not know how to respond to this. The usual reply of, "ew, cooties!" just didn't seem appropriate.

But I was relieved. I was glad nobody could see us. In other words, I was glad we were breaking the rules of the reformatory by being invisible because if anybody saw that we were being invisible we'd be in big trouble because being invisible was against the rules so the only way to get away with being invisible was to do so while being invisible.

Am I giving you an idea of the kind of stress I was under? My heart was pounding a fast, steady rhythm, as if the inside of my chest was a lower-floor apartment with a house party going on. I could sense that I was standing at the border that led to insanity, and all my papers were in order.

Agent FG emerged from a dark alcove and smiled at us. She looked very out of place in this setting, but no one was paying any attention to her so of course she was also invisible. The cooties of invisibility were hiding all three of us. (I never thought I'd ever have cause to use an expression like "the cooties of invisibility," and I hope I never do again.)

"From what Cinderella told me, it sounds like your dad zapped Agent O back into the earthly realm, and that's great news" Agent FG said. "Now you've got to call your dad, but you also have to get Agent O on the phone, immediately."

"Call my dad?"

She held up a small flip device.

"It's a trans-dimensional cell phone," she said. "It is quite unstable and highly illegal. The call can only last for a few moments and then the phone burns up in your hand."

"I imagine that would kill the resale value, huh?" I said.

"Cellular trans-dimensional technology is new. A wizard who works for us gave this to me, and you'd better believe he didn't want to part with it. But it could be the key to getting Agent O back here and that can only help you."

"And I'll get to talk to my dad?"

"No, I'm afraid you can't speak with him. The minute he answers the phone, you have to put Dronezzz on the line so she can talk to Agent O."

"But I want to talk to my dad!"

"I know, but if Dronezzz talks to Agent O, it will lead to you being free from this place, and that's what you want, right?"

"It's the best way to go," Cinderella said. "If Agent O can talk to Dronezzz, he can figure out a way to bust us out of here. Trust me."

I wanted to trust Cinderella. But I wasn't sure if her crazy subversive plans would help me or be the cause of my destruction. Even though I had known Cinderella for two or three hours, I guess I didn't know her that well at all.

"Okay," I said, ending the argument I was having inside my own head. "I'll do as you say."

There was no enthusiasm in my voice. I was just going along with their wishes because it seemed easier than asserting myself. Did I mention that I'm a huge wuss?

Agent FG disappeared back into the shadows, then Cinderella and I emerged from our cloak of cooties (another phrase I hope I never have to say again). We walked through the general population area to where Dronezzz was sitting.

"Okay, Dronezzz, we're ready," Cinderella said.

Dronezzz was about to say something, but Cinderella put her finger to her lips and gestured for her to be quiet. Dronezzz complied, but she seemed sad that Cinderella didn't want her to say anything. I felt bad because Dronezzz had been one of the few girls in this place who had been nice to me. So I felt compelled to say, "Hope everything is okay with you, Dronezzz."

"Thanks," she replied. "I'm okay, but it's so hard to maintain my vegan lifestyle in this place. The thing about being vegan is…"

I never heard another word. I fell to the floor and was fast asleep.

But once again, falling into a Dronezzz-induced sleep enabled me to astral-project into the basement of my home.

My dad was questioning Agent O, who was seated in one of those hard backed chairs that I think are manufactured strictly for police interrogations. Dad poked a harsh light in his face. He was bursting with rage and he looked like he was ready to start killing indiscriminately. I began crying astral tears because I missed him so much.

Despite his appearance of impending rampage, my dad as usual was being a total professional. "You'd better get your story straight, you miserable tub of crap!" he said. "You haven't said anything yet that doesn't make me want to throw you in jail."

"My dear sir," Agent O said in regal and distinguished tone that made it seem like his vocal cords were looking down their nose at the world. "Everything I've told you is the absolute truth. Your daughter is in a Fairy Tale Reformatory in an alternate universe."

I wasn't at all surprised when my dad grabbed him by his lapels and shook him, kicking the chair across the floor. My dad didn't believe it when junkie-snitches told him they were clean, so he certainly wasn't about to believe a story that sounded like it was concocted by a person high on drugs.

Agent O winced and braced himself for the worst; he looked like he was sure my dad was about to rearrange his face into a Picasso painting. But that is not my dad's way. He is much more into the threat of violence than actual violence. Dad's goal is to make a suspect soil himself with fear and reveal everything without ever finding out that physical harm was not part of the plan.

"You'd better tell me something that makes sense, or I'm going to stop being such a nice guy," Dad barked.

"Think about what's happened!" Agent O responded, somehow maintaining his cool in the midst of my dad's crazy rouge cop performance art. "I disappeared before your very eyes. Then you pressed a key on an iPad and I emerged in your basement out of nowhere. Things are happening that are beyond human understanding, but that doesn't mean I can't help you find your daughter. She is in grave danger and I can be of assistance."

Despite everything I just told you about my dad, for a minute there I thought he was going to slug Agent O. The logic behind his lack of logic was infuriating him. But after contemplating things for a moment, dad let go of his grip. Agent O took a moment to catch his breath. Dad was thinking hard, while never taking his eyes off of Agent O.

"I believe you are a complete lunatic," Dad said. "But if you can help me find my daughter, I'm listening."

Suddenly I felt like I was drowning. And then I opened my eyes and saw that Cinderella was throwing a cup of water in my face.

"Wake up!" she said. "You have to make that phone call."

Dronezzz now had a sock stuffed in her mouth. Cinderella didn't want her saying anything until she got on the phone with Agent O.

We went to a dark passageway where no one could see us. I was given the phone and I dialed my dad's cell. The phone rang once and then I head my dad say, "Hello? What? What?!!!"

It was joyous to hear his voice and I was about to scream into the phone how much I loved and missed him, but then Cinderella grabbed the phone from me, put the receiver to her ear and said, "Put the ogre on the phone." Then she pulled the sock from Dronezzz's mouth, handed her the phone and then roughly pushed me out of the passageway.

"What are you doing?" I said.

"We've got to get away from Dronezzz. If you overhear her speak it'll send you back to sleep."

"I wanted to speak to my dad!" I said.

"I told you, we have to get Dronezzz on the phone with Agent O. We have to think about what's best for the plan!"

"Plan?"

"Yes, the plan. You know, where you assassinate the Prince during brunch."

"I thought the plan was to get us out of here."

"Yeah, that too. After you kill the Prince. That's the plan."

"I agreed to no such plan!"

"What's the matter?" Cinderella said. "It sounds like you don't want to kill the Prince."

"Of course I don't want to kill the Prince!" I said. "I'm no assassin! I'm not even good at dodgeball!"

"But don't you see? I'm not invited to the Prince's Brunch. You are. So you're the one that has to kill him. It's the only way to bring justice and freedom to the Fairy Tale realm."

"Cinderella," I said. "I'm very fond of you, but you and your Fairy Godmother are insane!"

And, as if to prove my point, I could see Agent FG at the end of that dark hallway flailing her arms and talking to herself. Maybe I was a good judge of insanity.

But Cinderella and I were not on the same page, even though we were in the same book. "The Prince is a fascist dictator!" she said

"I'm sick of hearing this! Leave me alone!"

We were making a scene. Everyone was looking at us, including Dr. Strepgoat, who was peering down from an overhead catwalk. He smiled and gave me a thumbs-up sign.

Cinderella saw this.

"Oh, I get it," she said. "You're colluding with the enemy now."

"No!" I protested.

"You're on their side now," Cinderella said, the hurt and anger in her voice sticking into me like an ice pick.

"I'm not on anyone's side," I said, tears filling my eyes. "I just want to go home."

"We all do," Cinderella said. "We all do."

She gave me one last look of disdain, then turned around and walked away.

I could see Strepgoat smiling his approval. My chances of getting home seemed better than ever.

Then why was I so miserable?

CHAPTER FOURTEEN

I wandered through the reformatory in a sad daze. I ended up in the main common area, which consisted of randomly placed wooden tables and benches that termites had already had their way with. But it was the walls of peeling paint chips, and asbestos hanging like clouds on the ceiling that added just the right touch of biohazard toxicity to the room.

And speaking of toxicity, most of the other girls were gathered in groups excitedly discussing the Prince's Brunch. I was being ignored, which was fine with me.

But then a voice called out, "Hey, what's up?"

At first I didn't respond because it never occurred to me that the question was being directed at me.

"Hello? Parallel Universe of Earth to Laura!"

I glanced over to discover Concretia, gazing at me with a smile that looked like an intruder on her face; it must have had to bypass a security system to get there.

"Are you talking to me?" I said in a meant-to-be-menacing voice that wasn't so much Taxi Driver as Pony Rider.

"Yeah, I am talking to you," she said. "I heard you got accepted to the Prince's Brunch."

"Word gets around fast."

"I also heard you're no longer friends with Cinderella."

I didn't say anything. I had no interest in talking about this.

"Don't be so glum, things are looking up for you," she said. "If you're going to the Prince's Brunch, you must be pretty cool."

"I don't feel the least bit cool," I said.

She had made a bad first impression when she tried to kill me with her hair. But now she was being nice and I was conflicted because I tend to appreciate it when people are nice. It makes me want to be nice back. It's a Minnesota thing. But this was so out of the blue I didn't trust what was happening.

"Let's hang out for a while," she said. She motioned for me to sit next to her and I sat down because I just didn't have the energy to be rude.

"We can do fun stuff to get ready for the Prince's Brunch," she said. "Just like a couple of girly girl pals preparing for our big dates."

If she had been this way towards me when I first arrived, I would have been totally down for doing the giggly girly friendship thing, which was a phenomenon I had heard about and always wanted to try. But something about this just didn't feel right.

"I've got a fun idea!" she said. "Let's braid each other's hair!"

I didn't know how the hell I was supposed to braid the asphalt jungle that she called her hair; a power drill or a jackhammer were the only possible ways to go about it, and if I had those tools I would have been using them to try and break out of the reformatory.

"Uh, Concretia, this sounds like a lot of fun, but I have very little experience with beauty products and more to the point, considering the state of your hair, I have even less experience in the construction industry."

"Well, I admit, braiding my hair does require a certain skill-set that you might not have," she said. "But I just wanted to show my support for you."

As she said this to me, she was looking over my shoulder. I turned around and saw that she was making eye contact with Dr. Strepgoat, who was watching us from across the room. He seemed to be prodding her on. That's when I knew that Dr. Strepgoat had put her up to this.

"Gotta go!" I said, abruptly getting up and going. I had somehow found the strength to be rude.

I walked no further than a few feet when my path was blocked by Lunchabelle. Her eyes were opened wide with the intensity of a religious fanatic who was seeing God and then immediately being served a restraining order by Him. At first I thought she was sweating, but she wasn't sweaty so much as juicy. All sorts of greasy drippings and consommé were falling from her body. She was the first girl I ever met who made her own gravy.

"Hi," she said. "Can I ask you a favor?"

"Uh… I guess?"

"Come with me."

We stepped over to a slightly less populated part of the room, and as we walked I almost slipped on the liquids that dripped from her skin and formed puddles on the floor.

"I believe I can trust you," she said. "You see, you're the only girl here that I feel can resist having me for supper. I did some research into the nature of the world from whence you came, and I was surprised to find that people in your dimension as a general rule don't eat other people, at least not that often."

This was true. The human race can take pride in knowing that cases of cannibalism are mostly restricted to certain serial killers, a few frontiersmen caught in snowstorms, and perhaps a soccer player or two.

"It's mostly witches that I have to worry about," she said. "They're the ones who eat children and teenagers and there are no laws that protect kids like me from becoming cuisine against our will."

I felt bad for her. Growing up in a fairy tale kingdom is especially hard on the precociously mouth-watering.

"You're the only person here that I am confident will not eat me."

"Well, your confidence is well placed," I said. "When it comes to food my people try to avoid, human flesh is second only to carbs."

"That's why you're the only person I can ask to do this."

"Do what?"

"Could you please baste me?" she said, holding up a turkey baster. "In the current state I'm in, I need to be constantly basted or my skin will go dry and I'll get all itchy and wrinkled. I become overheated whenever I get excited and I'm totally psyched because I was approved to go to the Prince's Brunch. It's so refreshing to attend brunch rather than to be brunch. And maybe the Prince will like me and become my boyfriend. That would be awesome!"

Wow. She had some crazy notion that if only a devastatingly handsome guy liked her and became romantically smitten, her life would become so much better and all her problems would be solved. I knew this was a crazy idea because I had come up with it first.

She thrust the turkey baster towards me and I felt like I had no choice but to baste her. I figured I'd do it for just a few minutes, because it was just plain weird, especially after she started spinning around and around as if she was on a rotisserie.

As this was happening, I purposely looked away and tried to get my mind on something besides the task of helping another girl stay moist and tender. I looked over at a glass partition where we girls were monitored from a safe distance. I saw Cinderella's stepmother and stepsisters — Lanolin and Liceeta — talking with Dr. Strepgoat. They were all friendly and animated and full of smiles. It made me sick.

And what's worse, in the midst of all the laughing and smiling, Dr. Strepgoat caught my eye and smiled at me. Then Lanolin and Liceeta saw me, and I was horrified to see a total lack of contempt in their gazes, as if now they wanted to be friends. These nasty princesses of pain thinking well of me was as strong an indictment of my character as I could think of.

"I'm sorry, I can't baste you right now," I said to Lunchabelle. "I'll see you later, be sure to throughly wash your hands during preparation of yourself. Gotta run!"

I had to get away from everyone. Some of the people in this place were evil. Some of them were just deeply disturbed. But what really worried me was that it was starting to feel like the first place where I ever truly fit in.

CHAPTER FIFTEEN

I went looking for Cinderella. I wanted to make her understand that I needed to do what I had to do because if I didn't do what I needed to do I'd never be able to do what I wanted to do, which was to go home where I needed to be.

That's perfectly understandable, right?

But then I saw Cinderella being led away by two Sentries. Her hands and feet were manacled in chains so she was having a hard time walking, and the Sentries were moving her along at a fast clip, which made it doubly awkward and uncomfortable for her.

I almost couldn't look at her, I was so ashamed, but our eyes met and she said, "How do you like my new jewelry?"

She smiled her usual trouble-making smile. It was the Cinderella I knew, never letting her adversaries think they had the upper hand, even when they so clearly and so obviously had the upper hand.

"Where are they taking you?" I asked, walking beside her and trying to keep up.

"Oh, they're just hiding me away while the Prince is here. They don't want him seeing me, which is a weird coincidence, because I don't want to see him either."

Then she said, "I'm sorry I got mad at you. You need to keep your distance from me. I get it. It's my fault that you're here. I was asking too much of you. Take care, Laura."

They led her further away. I wanted to either hug her, or bash in the heads of the Sentries that were treating her in such a rough manner. Of course, I would never bash in the heads of anyone, so hugging her was the better option, but unfortunately I wasn't able to do that either.

I was so relieved that Cinderella wasn't mad at me anymore, but I was also in a real funk. I felt so sorry for Cinderella, but to be honest, I felt even sorrier for myself. I didn't think I'd ever snap out of this awful state of…

Oh, my God, look at this incredible gown I'm wearing!

That was my immediate thought because at that moment, a witchy matron, different from the one that had earlier lost her mind in a fit of unauthorized romanticism, was waving a wand at various girls and suddenly out of nowhere I was decked out like some sort of princess.

The gown I was wearing was long and flowing and lacy and soft and, yes, a little scratchy and a bit unwieldy, but I didn't care. I loved the way I looked.

Plus, I now had a hairdo that could have been coifed at some high-end salon, and I was wearing makeup that hid all my imperfections. I have no idea what those imperfections are, and I couldn't point them out if you asked me, so of course I was glad to be rid of them.

Okay, I admit it: I'm not immune to this princess stuff. I know that on a higher level, it's shallow, the kind of thing a person of depth and substance would have no interest in. But it was only at this moment that I understood why some people have no interest in depth and substance. I realize this is an awful thing to say, but it might be the case that the only happy people in the world are shallow people. So I couldn't help it, I was embracing my inner-superficiality.

All of us newly minted princesses were instructed to stand at the front of the room in a line. Dr. Strepgoat arrived and surveyed us. The increased elegance of his surroundings did nothing to diminish his usual douchebag demeanor.

"Listen up, ladies," he said. "First of all, keep one thing in mind: you are not princesses! Not in the least bit. Not even remotely. You just look like princesses, but deep down you are still the same worthless juvenile delinquents you've always been. All of the couture in the world will not change that!"

He always had such a charming way of putting things.

"Furthermore," he continued. "There are certain rules and regulations you are going to have to obey or you will be in much bigger trouble than ever, I'm not kidding!"

I won't go into detail about the protocols we had to follow, but the list was long, and the restrictions numerous. We were only supposed to nod and curtsey when spoken to by the Prince. Sweet, smiling submission was the order of the day. Any words or deeds that even vaguely resembled a individual personality would be considered a major infraction.

His whole spiel emphasized what Cinderella had been saying about the Prince's regime: it was a fascist dictatorship. And in a way, all us girls being excited about dressing in identical sparkly gowns was proof of how all of us were only too willing to fall under the thumb of conformity. And that's just the type of thing that can lead to authoritarian governments.

But da-um, I looked good!

(This type of self-aggrandizing bravado was not at all typical of me, which is why I was embracing it so enthusiastically.)

The embarrassing truth is, it felt good to feel frivolous. My life had been heavy and hard for so long, what with all the tragedy and isolation and social incompetence. As senseless as it was, this heavy gown had lightened my mood.

We were now marched in single file to the dining hall, which was decorated to look like a room in a castle as opposed to the dingy cafeteria it was. But since we really weren't in a castle, the décor had the effect of making the room look like a cheesy chain restaurant with a medieval theme. I half expected a kid with an "assistant manager" name-tag on polyester knight's armor to ask if I wanted fries with my order.

There were horn-playing Sentries decked out in velvet dink-wear, fancier than usual plastic silverware, and delicately embroidered napkins that would never be caught dead in the vicinity of barbecue sauce.

There were also visitors, or as they would prefer to be called, dignitaries. Among them were Cinderella's stepmother and stepsisters. They sat behind a long banquet table up on an elevated platform facing the tables that all us elegantly dressed low-life girl-scum would be sitting at.

But then everybody stood, because there was a blaring of horns, a beating of drums and an excited gasp from all the wretched waifs, myself included.

The Prince had arrived.
CHAPTER SIXTEEN

Oh my God, the Prince was handsome. I'm talking Gil Davis-level handsome. You know, the guy at school that I almost made eye contact with? You know, my hypothetical soul-mate for life? You know, my wild, passionate, impromptu relationship that's still in the prospectus stage? Yeah, that guy, the one I'm on a first-name basis with, as in, I totally know his first name.

And the Prince was just as hot, although Gil Davis is more of an alt-indie version of a fairy tale prince, with a gangly body perfect in its awkwardness, unruly jet black hair, brown skin that expands the concept of "Minnesotan" in the most awesome way, and intense eyes that I'm sure are some dazzling shade of blue or green, but to be honest I've never been close enough to them to say for sure.

The Prince had one other thing in common with Gil Davis — he was fictional. I mean, even though I see Gil Davis in person five days a week, he's still mainly a figment of my imagination. We've only hung out with each other inside the confines of my own mind, so he's pretty much a Gil Davis I've adapted into a mental screenplay based on a Gil Davis from another medium — Real Life.

Maybe if I always dressed as I was dressed at that moment, I could have had the courage to have a conversation with Gil Davis. If nothing else, he might have said, "Hey, aren't you a bit overdressed for study hall?" and that would have at least been an icebreaker. I think that for shy social misfits like myself, starting a conversation always seems a daunting, insurmountable task, fraught with peril. I consider myself a person with a vast knowledge of certain topics; there's a lot I could say. Yet when I meet a stranger, especially one I want to get to know, the best I can come up with is something like, "nice weather we're having." It's a boring way to start a discussion, and in Minnesota it's almost never true.

But now here I was standing not far from the Prince, a dreamy guy from a dream world, a whole other plane of existence, so I wondered if maybe the tightness I feel in my gut whenever the ones I yearn for inevitably walk away from me, completely oblivious to my presence, will not seem as real to me in this world of fantasy. Of course, it was crazy of me to think that, because the threat to my life that I was experiencing felt as real and as terrifying as anything I had ever felt in my normal existence. But I wasn't contemplating matters of life and death; I was thinking about the everyday threats to my spirit that happen in the course of my regular mundane routine on the planet earth: a curt look, a mean quip, or any kind of verbal ridicule feels like it can cause permanent scaring, and then I don't end up meeting or talking to anyone, because I'm confined to a quarantine burn ward of my own making.

Jeez. It would nice if my mind wasn't a dark labyrinth of insecurity with no exit in sight, but alas, it is, so I sarcastically thought to myself, "I bet you're fun at parties," and then I remembered, holy crap, I am at a party!

All of us faux-princess prisoners stood in a line as the Prince walked down the aisle and took a slight look at each of us. He showed all the passion of a man examining showroom furniture. We all basically looked identical and his polite smile stayed exactly the same as he passed each of us.

Every girl on line stood at attention, but the eyes on every face were burning like trash fires in the middle of a vacant lot. No one was allowed to speak unless spoken to, yet in their expressions, everyone still managed to silently say, "Pick me! Pick me!"

As a matter or polite protocol, the Prince did stop and talk to a few of us girls.

"So, how is everything working out for you?" he said to Lunchabelle.

"I... I'm fine, thank you," she said.

Her proximity to the Prince was turning Lunchabelle into a bouillabaisse of stress.

"I've been briefed about you," he said. "You're Lunchabelle, are you not?"

"Yes, I am," she replied. As she said this, her lips made crackling sounds like extra-well-done burgers on a restaurant grill that had yet to receive a grade from the health department.

"I know your brother, Lunchabill," the Prince said. "Nice guy."

At this point I thought Lunchabelle might combust into a grease fire. But she kept perfectly still with that same anguished smile slathered on her face. She calmly said, "Your highness, my brother set me up to take the fall and I'm innocent. He's a snitch, a sniveling weasel."

"Lovely meeting you," the Prince said, continuing down the line, leaving Lunchabelle to stand in place. All of the short-order sizzling on her body stopped. The mention of her brother had put an abrupt end to her pining for the Prince. She was over him. The kitchen was closed.

"My, what unique hair," the Prince said, stopping to talk to Concretia.

"It's awesome, isn't it, your highness?" she said. "It's just another sign of your amazing greatness that you realize how amazingly great my hair is."

"Yes, indeed," the Prince said, already starting to move away from her.

"Go ahead and break ground on me if you'd like," she said.

The Prince was being extra courteous when he said, "I must be moving on."

He was still smiling, but the Sentries began pointing their weapons in Concretia's direction, so she was aware that her moment had passed.

I knew that Concretia was a troubled person, prone to follicle-based violence, but I think what made the Prince and his minions wary was the self-confidence she was showing; she was acting as if she was worthy of the Prince's affections and deserving of his time. Not cool with these dudes. Not cool at all.

Finally, the Prince came upon me. He didn't give me a second glance, because his first glance was all it took to get him to talk to me.

"Who are you?" he asked.

"I'm Laura," I said. It was touch and go there for a moment, but despite my being so flustered, I did somehow manage to remember my name.

"There is a bit of a foreign cadence to your voice," he said. "I find it quite enchanting."

He looked me directly in the eyes and smiled. Just as I had predicted, making eye-contact with a man-babe was something I enjoyed. It made my entire body feel warm, like the soothing comfort of a heating blanket just before it short circuits into an electrical fire.

Somehow, I managed to say, "I'm from a place called Minnesota."

"Well," he said. "If everyone from Minnesota is as lovely as you are, it must be a beautiful place indeed."

"Just don't go there in February," I said.

There was a collective gasp from everyone around me.

"How dare you tell the Prince where he should or shouldn't go!" Dr. Strepgoat said.

I have to admit there was a bit of a trace of personality in my voice. It was the type of innocently glib thing anyone would say to anyone else, so I knew right away I had made a mistake.

But the Prince's delighted expression had not changed. "Please, my dear, tell me," he said. "Why should I not go there in February?"

I was now at the point where I just wanted to get this conversation over with before I was punished for the capitol offense of responding to small talk with more small talk, so I just blurted out, "Because you'll freeze your ass off."

This produced an even bigger gasp, and Strepgoat motioned for the Sentries to take me away. But then I heard a piercing laugh, the kind of laugh Satan would use to con his way into a church picnic. I wondered where it was coming from and then I realized it was the Prince who was making this happy, albeit disturbing, sound.

"You are truly beguiling," he said. I looked around to see who he was talking to, but believe it or not, he was talking to me. "I think that before we eat our brunch, we should have a a dance. Would you care to?"

My knees went offline. I could barely stand, much less move, much less dance. No one had ever asked me to dance before. I didn't quite know what to say or do, but I somehow conjured the word, "Yes," which to my relief turned out to be the correct answer.

I may have been disliked by all the other girls before, but now I had committed the unpardonable sin of being appealing to the Prince.

Having other girls jealous of me was a new experience, because I had never before done anything that anyone could possibly be jealous of.

The Prince led me away from the line to the "dance floor," which is just a euphemism for some space between the tables.

I saw the looks on the other girl's faces. They were the kinds of facial expressions you never see at the center of an event; you see them on the periphery of things; it's the body language of the outlier, always squinting to see what's going on, as if trying to make out the smallest letters on an eye chart, always just out of earshot, never cc'd on anything cool and exciting that might be happening. Not participants in life so much as participants in the comments section of life.

If the other girls felt jealousy towards me, it was something I understood. I think that in a lot of cases, jealousy isn't even mean-spirited, it's just a natural way of being. For some reason wanting things is so much harder when other people are having things.

I knew what that felt like because I had been jealous many times in my past. I had never seen myself as the girl on the dance floor, I always saw myself as the girl on the sidelines of the dance floor, serving refreshments, and not even edgy enough to spike the punch bowl with Diet Shasta.

And now, here I was, the belle of the brunch. But I was quickly realizing that the only way I could enjoy being the center of attention was if everybody stopped looking at me.

CHAPTER SEVENTEEN

The Prince and I began to dance. I not sure, but I think we were waltzing. I had never met anyone who had waltzed before, but I recognized it as the kind of thing people in powered wigs did in old black & white movies. I always found it odd that after spinning around and around so much they didn't throw up, but I somehow managed to avoid any projectile vomiting, so I guess it turns out I'm good at waltzing. Who knew?

My feet moved in exactly the right steps to exactly the right rhythm, totally in synch with the Prince and his steps and his rhythm.

Now, you may be wondering: what rhythm? There was no music playing even though there were musicians nearby – thin boney men dressed like Buckingham Palace guards who played long horns with flags draped on them. But they didn't dare play a note. The musical style they worked in was mostly fanfares that announced the arrival and/or departure of the Prince. As far as I could tell, none of the musicians in this "band" knew any "songs" that lasted more than a few seconds or so. My point is that if you're having a wedding or a bar mitzvah or any kind of event in the fairy tale kingdom, you're better off hiring a DJ.

The Prince and I danced for a second, or an eternity, I'm not sure. All I know is, the experience of dancing with a cute guy was something completely new to me, and it made me giddy. Or psychotic. Maybe both, I'm not sure. But the Prince seemed to be enjoying himself. He smiled right at me and I want to say his smile was like a massage to my heart, but anytime a person's heart is being massaged, it usually means they're having cardiac surgery, so this wasn't like that at all. I'm just saying that the Prince's smile made me feel good in a way that other things, like for instance, reality, didn't measure up to.

Yes, I still knew that the Prince was the monarch of an awful regime. And yet I was hoping he'd ask me out. I was discovering that in certain situations, hotness and hormones take precedence over reason and rationality.

The Prince and I simultaneously stopped dancing, as if the song we were both hearing inside our heads had come to a halt and ending the dance was the most natural thing in the world. I think this is what they mean by chemistry between two people. Whatever that music was, it was our song. And it was not something you could ever download off of iTunes, it could only be downloaded from our hearts, but I can't say for sure whether or not you'd be charged 99 cents for it. You can't put a price on love, although I just did, so I guess putting a price on love is exactly the kind of crazy thing you do when true love – the kind you just can't put a price on – is happening to you.

I know what I'm saying isn't making much sense but I was dizzy and I don't think I wanted anything to make sense.

"Let us have brunch!" the Prince declared, and Dr. Strepgoat gave all the girls the signal to sit down in their seats at the long tables.

I was about to go back to my assigned seat, but the Prince said, "Would you do me the honor of dining with me?"

"Of course, I would love to dine with you, your highness," I said. "But it is you who are doing me the honor."

Then, showing a sudden sense of social grace that had eluded me for my entire sixteen years in the known world, I curtseyed with delicate precision.

That's right, I curtseyed.

Such an act seen in the regular teenage world that I came from would have banned me from every clique and cool peer group in high school. In other words, it would have kept things status quo. A curtesy in the twenty-first century is an engraved invitation to a life of not getting engraved invitations to anything ever. But here, in this world of waltzes and whatnot, it was a smooth move. Socially, I was hitting it out of the ballpark, although I was now too classy to ever be in a ballpark.

I don't know what came over me. I guess it might be that I was only a graceful person on paper, and since I was living inside a storybook, what worked on paper was working for me in practice. It's a theory, anyway.

"You're doing great," Strepgoat whispered to me as I went to sit down in my seat next to the Prince. "Your problems will soon be over."

I could tell that Strepgoat was genuinely pleased. I was clicking with the Prince, and that meant Strepgoat was pleasing him, so it wasn't too far-fetched to think that he would repay me and my situation would improve dramatically.

So as I sat down and brunch was served, I was thinking that falling in love with a handsome prince might actually have its good side.

The food was much better than the slop I had gotten at my previous reformatory meal. It didn't smell like dog doo and it didn't make me want to Heimlich myself, so I was sure this meal had been catered.

The Prince ate but I didn't hear him chew. I think chewing was beneath him and my guess was that the moment the food entered his mouth it genuflected and then silently tiptoed down his throat.

I was self-conscious eating in front of such a refined person. The food on my plate was either a Cornish Game Hen, or perhaps a mythical beast that went well with au jus sauce, I wasn't sure. But the main thing I focused on was staring at the Prince's beautiful face and not eating with my mouth open. I think I was successful because I didn't spit or drool on him as I ate, and I have reason to believe that not spitting and not drooling on your dining partner while you eat would go under the general heading of good table manners.

I didn't talk much during the meal. I mainly smiled and nodded when the Prince spoke. He mostly said mundane stuff like, "Lovely weather we're having" (the reigning box-office champ of small talk), and "I think this reformatory is helping you girls quite a bit," and also, "Would you please be a dear and make-out with me? It would be ever so enchanting."

(Well, to be honest, he didn't say that last thing, but I was imagining him saying something like that.)

The meal ended and the Prince stood and addressed the room.

"You have all been lovely and charming company," he said. "I think this reformatory is a monument to the idea of female rehabilitation. Don't forget that this institution is here to help you achieve what should be your ultimate goal: to become mere shells of your former selves. So I want to thank you all for a delightful brunch."

I was getting ready to go back in line with the other girls, but then the Prince firmly held my hand and said, "Right now I'd like to give this especially fine young fair maiden something."

A fair maiden? Me?

One of the Prince's assistants handed him a shoebox. He opened it, revealing a glass slipper that shined in the afterglow of a thorough windexing.

"I wanted to see if you would fit into this," he said, gazing straight into my eyes with a look of adoration that I hadn't seen on his face since a few minutes earlier, when he glanced at a mirror.

"This is the glass slipper that I put on Cinderella's foot," the Prince said. "I'm just curious to see if your foot would fit into it."

At that moment, Cinderella's stepsister, Liceeta, who had been looking on from the VIP dais, limped forward and said, "I think I can fit into the glass slipper now, your highness. I've cut off two more of my toes since the last time you saw me. I didn't tell you right away because I wanted my latest decapitation to be a special surprise!"

The stepmother pulled Liceeta back into her seat. She knew that her cause with the Prince was doomed, and that if her daughter was going to continue to chop off limbs, she would have to do it for personal fulfillment, and not as a way to win over the Prince, because that train had left the station, and she was already limping and moving too slow to ever catch that train.

After the awkwardness of the moment passed, the Prince returned his attention to me. He got on blended knee and presented the glass slipper with an elegance that went way beyond anything I had ever experienced at Lady Foot Locker. "Please," he said. "Try this on."

I removed one of the perfectly fine fancy dress shoes that had been magic-wanded onto my feet. I placed my right foot into the slipper.

It fit perfectly.

"Congratulations," the Prince said. "You are now officially the new

Cinderella."

CHAPTER EIGHTEEN

The new Cinderella? What the hell did that mean? Regardless, this news caused an uproar among everyone around me.

Dr. Strepgoat squeaked, honked and moonwalked, and it was every bit as reprehensible as you might imagine.

Concretia, in a somewhat less joyous mood, banged her head on the table, which caused damage to both her hair and the table.

Cinderella's stepsisters, Liceeta and Lanolin, burst into tears, and I felt sorry for them. A lifetime of bad advice and negativity from a nasty parent had somehow resulted in extreme unhappiness. Go figure.

Lunchabelle's anger towards the Prince bubbled over in the form of spicy overheated sweat that splashed on the girls sitting around her, but they didn't even notice because they were too caught up in the excitement of something they were required by law to be excited about.

I admit, it did seem exciting, but I had to say it out loud: "What do you mean by 'a new Cinderella?'"

"I field this one, your highness, if I may?" Strepgoat said. He then turned and addressed his remarks directly to me: "The story of Cinderella is very important to the world. Not just your world, but all the worlds in all the universes where the storybooks that convey our fairy tale way of life have been published, and we get a percentage of the money from every book sold. It's what helps finance the Royal Kingdom."

"Really?"

"Yes. That's why they're called royalties."

I really don't think that's why they're called that, but I knew better than to contradict him.

"The stories in our world repeat themselves over and over again, so that each generation can experience the stories anew," he continued. "The Cinderella that you recently met comes from a long line of Cinderellas. Each Cinderella of each generation lives out the same story that the previous generation's Cinderella lived. That way the tale can be retold and put into a storybook form and become available wherever books are sold."

So far he had been talking with the upbeat cadence of an infomercial pitchman telling a story that closes the sale every time. Then his tone changed, becoming dark and bitter.

"But this generation's Cinderella ruined the Cinderella story," he said. "She defied the conventions of the Kingdom. She rejected the Prince and turned her back on a storybook ending. This is something that must be repaired."

"The whole purpose of this brunch was to see if I could find a new Cinderella," the Prince added.

"Hello? I'm perfectly capable of being Cinderella!" Liceeta cried out.

Because of her previous outburst, it was no surprise to hear Liceeta say this, but it was a bit jarring when her sister, Lanolin, stood up and said. "No! No! No! I'm the new Cinderella! I can alter my body even more to make it happen! I can!"

She suddenly pulled out a switchblade and began cutting her ear off. Even in the oftentimes-horrific world of fairy tales, this was a bit much. Blood started streaming down her neck and covering her dress like gruesome gravy stains.

"See!" she screamed. "I'm pretty enough to be Cinderella!!! I'm pretty enough!!!"

Okay, clearly her brain had entered an asylum that had an empty room available, and several Sentries grabbed her and her sister and their stepmother and pulled them all out of the room. They never had the chance to thank the Prince for his gracious hospitality.

It was now a full-on horror movie, and I like horror movies, but I was flustered by everything that was going on. I didn't know how to process it, and I was regretting that I had to watch Lanolin disfigure herself right after I had just eaten.

But the Prince, in the midst of it all, remained as calm and affable as ever.

"I'll be honest with you," he said to me. "I organized this brunch the minute I heard that an alien from another dimension had entered our world and that she was so lovely."

Oh my God. Was he calling me lovely? I didn't necessarily disagree with him, but I wasn't used to hearing it said out loud.

"You see, every fair maiden in the kingdom had already tried on the glass slipper," the Prince said. "So I just had to see if the attractive new undocumented intruder would fit into the slipper."

I liked the part where he said I'm attractive.

I know that people can became hooked on all sorts of things – drugs, alcohol, cigarettes, cupcakes – but it looked like I was becoming addicted to positive reinforcement.

"And now that you have fit into the slipper," the Prince said. "You are qualified to be the new Cinderella. And I am officially in love with you!"

Trumpets blared. No, really, the horn players lifted up their instruments and played that one short fanfare song they knew, which I wasn't sure was an original or a cover.

"True Love has returned to the Fairy Tale Kingdom," the Prince declared. "There is much to celebrate!"

Well, yes and no. Living happily ever after was fine and all, but I didn't want to live happily ever after in this place. I wanted to go home.

But then Strepgoat came over to me and whispered in my ear (an ear I was grateful I still had having just witnessed Lanolin's outburst), "If you play your cards right, and just be the new Cinderella for as long as it takes to record the whole thing so that it can be entered into the chronicle of happily-ever-after fairy tale mythology, I'll see to it that you get back to your world. This is a win/win for you."

"I don't understand," I said. "How can I live happily ever after in a fairy tale kingdom and still go home?"

He pulled me further to the side and whispered, "The happily ever after thing only lasts until the last page of the book when it says, '...And they lived happily ever after.' After that, the royal marriage is secretly annulled and each Cinderella has her memory erased and then is sent away from the castle to live anonymously among the peasants. That's what happened to Cinderella's mother, the previous Cinderella, although she had no idea that she had once been a Princess."

"Their memories are erased?"

"Yeah, the wizards and sorcerers always used to concoct a spell that would make each Cinderella forget that she had been Cinderella. Then she'd go off into the world, marry some commoner schmuck, give birth to a daughter, and then that daughter would be in line to become the next Cinderella for the next Prince. The new Cinderella would be thrown into the same situation as before with an evil stepmother and evil stepsisters after her own mother had died of quote, 'natural causes.'"

He laughed the kind of laugh only a person with no sense of humor laughs, leaving no doubt that there was nothing natural about the causes that killed Cinderella's real mother.

"But here's the beauty part," Strepgoat said. "In your case, once your happily-ever-after moment reaches its last page, we'll just send you back to your world, so like I said, it's a total win for you."

This was disturbing news, but if it meant I could go home, then I was totally onboard. I still didn't understand why it was such a big deal that my foot fit into the glass slipper. I had never worn the slipper before and I had never danced with the Prince until this very day, so what did it matter if I fit into the slipper?

And yet, because I fit into the slipper, the Prince announced that he was in love with me. Why? It made no sense. It's almost as if there's no rationality or reason when it comes to love.

Whatever. My attitude was: let's just get this over with so I can return to my regular life.

But then I remembered an important detail. "What's going to happen to Cinderella?" I asked.

"Oh, this will delight you," Strepgoat said. "She is finally going to achieve true happiness."

And at that moment, the old Cinderella, or should I say, my Cinderella, *the*

Cinderella, was led into the room.

She was still chained up and now her mouth was covered with one of those Handmaid's Tale gags. Not a good sign.

"This will be the perfect way to inaugurate the new lobotomy wing of our institution," Strepgoat said. "The wizards and sorcerers have achieved so many advancements in personality-extraction technology since the days of the previous Cinderellas. But this particular Cinderella requires special treatment. We will transition her into a harmless vegetative state."

"And then Laura can begin her life as the new Cinderella," the Prince said.

Cinderella's eyes met mine. They were pleading and hopeless.

I desperately wanted to help her, but if I did, I'd never get home, and I really, really, really wanted to go home.

At that moment Cinderella's Fairy Godmother came into view and I breathed a sigh of relief. Perhaps Agent FG could solve all this. If she was so brazenly showing herself in the main part of the Reformatory, maybe that meant she had a bold plan and was ready to finally bring down the Prince once and for all.

But then she held up one of those musket-like weapons, pointed it straight at Cinderella's head, and addressed the Prince. "Everything is working out perfectly, your highness," she said. "Just as we planned it."

Oh, crap.

CHAPTER NINETEEN

Agent FG seemed quite satisfied with herself as she helped Strepgoat attach Cinderella to the lobotomy device, a spider-like contraption of straps and wires hanging from the wall.

"You see, Laura," she said. "Agent O and I do work for a secret organization, but it's not against the monarchy. We work for the monarchy."

She said this casually as she and Strepgoat chained Cinderella's hands above her head.

"We did send that e-book out to the mortal world to bring someone to our world, not to break Cinderella out of jail, but to provide the Prince with the new Cinderella that he needed."

A gigantic metallic pincushion-type device with what looked like porcupine needles sticking out was lowered and moved towards Cinderella's head.

Agent FG rubbed Cinderella's hair from her eyes and stared at her with the kind of smug self-satisfaction that only those unworthy of smug self-satisfaction are capable of. If Cinderella hadn't been gagged, a torrent of four-letter insults and every other letter-combination of insults would have no doubt spewed from her lips.

"You just couldn't play along, could you, Cinderella?" Agent FG said. "You couldn't live out your life in the preordained scenario that had been written for you. Properly behaved young ladies are supposed to go by the script, but you tried to write your own script and now you will pay the price."

Strepgoat flipped a switch and the pointy lobotomy device began spinning just inches from Cinderella's forehead. Her eyes widened with terror as it spun closer and closer to her.

The Prince nuzzled up to me as if we were watching an adorable rom-com on the Hallmark channel "I can't wait to take you to my castle," he cooed. "You are my true Cinderella and I am so delighted I found you. And as soon as we erase the old Cinderella's brain, you and I can begin a new chapter of happiness."

I turned and gazed into the Prince's eyes. Oh, man, those eyes were amazing. He was so good-looking. Such a total babe. The ultimate trophy-dude. So there was only one thing to do.

I pulled the glass slipper off my foot, smashed it against the wall, grabbed the Prince from behind, put him in a choke-hold, and held the glass shards of the slipper up to his cute handsome dreamy babelicious throat.

"Turn that lobotomy contraption off or I will shred the Prince's tonsils!" I yelled.

Every single mouth in the room went into instant agape mode. They all stared at me in with shock and disbelief. They couldn't believe what they were seeing. Hell, I was the one doing it and I couldn't believe it either!

"Do what I say or I will empty out his internal organs!" I screamed.

Yes, that's right, I screamed. I'm not normally a screamer; I tend to talk like an NPR station with the volume turned down. But I felt it was important to get my point across.

The Prince, who had an allergic reaction to assertive, take-charge woman, was afraid, very afraid. "Oh for heaven's sake, do as she says!" he pleaded in a tone of voice that was so wobbly it almost made me seasick to hear it.

"You're making a big mistake," Agent FG said to me. "You have no idea what you're dealing with."

"Shut up!" I said. "You're a lousy fairy godmother."

Wow. I had never so blatantly insulted anyone to their face like that before. I never even insult people behind their back. But in desperate times like these, good manners are about as appropriate as a poetry reading at a NASCAR race.

Despite what was happening, Dr. Strepgoat was still determined to continue kissing-up to the Prince no matter what. "I'm going to write you up for this, young lady," he said.

I had heard teachers at my school say this exact thing to other kids, but never to me. Also, judging by the way I was manhandling the Prince, it could not be denied that I was roughhousing in the hallway.

"Shut your goat-hole and release Cinderella," I replied. "Now!"

I was holding tight to the Prince's neck and his face was right up against mine. It was the closest I had ever been to him. It was like we were spooning in a totally deranged way. But any attraction I might have had to him before was now greatly diminished by his infantile whimpering. Coming from a puppy, or even a sensitive guy, this might be endearing, but coming from a fascist dictator, it was just pathetic. I almost said, "I can't believe I liked you," but I didn't, because I was ashamed to say it out loud. The promise of romance had caused me to seriously consider banishing the concept of right and wrong from my head. But that particular fever had broken.

It's kind of funny how I went so quickly from wanting the Prince to be my boyfriend to being more than willing to use him as a hostage. I guess the hard lesson that relationships can change on a dime was something I was learning faster than most.

Cinderella's gag was removed and she was released from her chains. She immediately grabbed one of those musket-like weapons from a Sentry and held it up to Agent FG's head.

"If you make one move to stop us, I'm going to magically transform your brain into a blood-splattered pumpkin!" she said.

"Cinderella, you're overreacting," Agent FG said in a nervous, fake-friendly tone. "You're acting as if being lobotomized against your will is a bad thing. But you should have an open mind about closing your mind."

"Shut up!" Cinderella said. "I agree with Laura. You're a crappy fairy godmother. If you ever try to be a fairy godmother to anyone else, you may not use me as a reference." She said this as she gagged her and used the same chains she had been bound with to chain Agent FG to the wall.

"What's our next move, Cinderella?" I asked.

"Well," she said. "My first move is to thank you for being such a pal."

"No problem," I replied. "I didn't want to be Cinderella anyway."

"Believe me, it's not all it's cracked up to be. Now let's get the hell out of here!"

She turned to Strepgoat. "Open the trans-dimensional portal!"

"I don't have the authority to do that," he said.

Cinderella pushed him against the wall till he was propped up on his hind hooves. He began making frightened squeaky sounds that I would have found heartbreaking coming from an actual goat, but coming from his weasly mouth, it was a beautiful kind of music to hear.

"For God's sake, do as she says!" the Prince pleaded. I wanted to let the Prince out of my grip as soon as I could, because I had the feeling he was going to piss his pants at any moment.

Still, I kept the broken glass slipper inches from the Prince's throat while Cinderella wedged the barrel of her weapon into the side of Strepgoat's skull. It was awkward to walk across the room while holding broken glass to a person's throat, but we still managed to make our way to the part of the reformatory where I had originally arrived.

We reached the exact spot of the wall where I had made my initial entrance into this fairy tale reformatory. All the other girls followed us like a crowd that was observing a potentially violent game of golf.

Cinderella faced the roomful of inmates and said, "Anyone who wants to break out of here with us is free to do so."

Surprisingly, all of the girls stayed right where they were. A prison reformatory may have been a miserable, torturous place, but it was a miserable torturous place they had gotten used to. Perhaps some felt that escaping into another world would just bring a new set of dangers, and considering what had happened to me, I couldn't deny they had a point.

There was only one other prisoner who joined us.

"I'm in," Concretia said, stepping forward.

"Concretia! I'm surprised at you!" Strepgoat said with his usual condescension.

"I've heard that hair helmets are a thing in the earthly world," she said. "I have a feeling that my hair will find an acceptance there that it's never had here."

This seemed like a weird reason to visit an alternate dimension, even for her. But Cinderella had made her offer to all the girls, so as apprehensive as we might have been about Concretia's trustworthiness, she was welcome to come along.

At Cinderella's command, Strepgoat pulled an iPad out of a bin. It looked like mine, the one that that was identical to the Ogre's iPad and had been confiscated when I first arrived. And this was confirmed when he pressed the # key and it shot out a lazar that cut into the wall, creating a passageway which led to the trans-dimensional portal.

"Could you please hold on to my iPad?" I asked Cinderella, since my hand were full at the moment with my royal hostage.

She took the tablet from Strepgoat and I could see that the battery was almost dead and that these enchanted apps were still wreaking havoc with my storage space. I doubted if these issues could be addressed at the Genius Bar.

As we ventured forth into the tunnel, the Prince pleaded, "You are on your way, please let me go."

Cinderella dismissed his plea with a laugh. "We're not letting anybody go until we're safely away from here," she said.

We were about to move forward when Lunchabelle emerged from the crowd. "I wanted to say goodbye before you left," she said.

"Why don't you come with us?" Cinderella asked.

"I need to stay here because of family obligations."

"Really?"

"Yes, I am obligated to stick around so I can seek a blood-soaked revenge against my brother, Lunchabill. But I wanted to thank you for not eating me."

She embraced Cinderella, which was a little awkward, because all the juices and grease dripping from Lunchabelle got all over her and on the floor, which caused Cinderella to lose her footing a bit.

This resulted in her briefly pointing her weapon away from Strepgoat, and then this gave Concretia the opportunity to slam the side of Cinderella's head with her hair and then grab the weapon from her.

She pointed the weapon at me and demanded, "Let the Prince go!"

"Oh, Concretia," I said. "This is why you're a horrible fairy tale character and nobody ever wants to read a book about you."

For a moment I was afraid she was going to use her hair to launch a blitzkrieg on my face. So I did the expedient thing, which was to release the Prince from my grip.

"Oh, bless you, dear girl," the Prince said to Concretia.

"I hope you realize that this makes me your new Cinderella," she said.

"Oh, of course! Of course!" the Prince said, as if he really meant it.

I couldn't believe Concretia believed him. Underneath that thick concrete head was an even thicker skull. I was about to tell her she was dumb to fall for this line, but then I remembered that I had just had my first boyfriend and it wasn't five minutes before I shoved a weaponized glass slipper up to his throat and was threatening to kill him, so who was I to be giving relationship advice?

As the Prince frantically sprung away from me, he couldn't help but slip on the puddle of grease that Lunchabelle had dripped onto the floor. He stumbled and fell towards Concretia, and landed in her arms. This made her smile, but it also made her forget that she was supposed to be keeping her gun trained on me. And this enabled Cinderella to push Strepgoat away from her and into Concretia and the Prince, sending them all plummeting downward. So now Concretia, the Prince and Strepgoat were on the ground.

I didn't know what to do, so I turned to Cinderella for some kind of well-thought-out master plan, and sure enough, she had one:

"Run!!!" she screamed.

And that's exactly what we did.

We ran into the trans-dimensional tunnel and we ran and ran and ran. And then ran some more.

It looked like we were making a clean escape. There was only one problem.

We had no idea where we were going. The battery on the iPad was almost dead, so there was no tractor-beam sound coming from it to guide us, and now we were lost in what seemed like an endless maze of psychedelic abstract imagery. And I was starting to get tired. All of this surrealism was exhausting.

Meanwhile, the Prince and Concretia and Strepgoat had gotten up off the floor and started chasing us.

Strepgoat was several paces ahead of Concretia and the Prince and he was gaining on us. I'll say this for him — being half man/half goat made him very fast when he needed to be.

So we stuck to our plan and kept running. Nothing lay ahead except darkness.

But then from that darkness a figure emerged. It looked like someone big and scary but I couldn't make out who it was. A demon from another dimension?

Yes, it was a demon from another dimension. My favorite demon from any dimension in any universe.

"Dad!" I cried.

CHAPTER TWENTY

Even when he's in familiar surroundings, my dad has a sour look on his face, like he's just eaten expired lunch meat. So as he stood in the middle of a kaleidoscopic trans-dimensional alternate universal interstate of mind highway, let's just say he was not in his comfort zone.

"What the hell is going on here?" he said in the irritable tone I knew and loved him for.

I rushed over and hugged him. My dad is not one to openly show affection for me or anyone else for that matter. He has a big heart, but it's always surrounded by "police line do not cross" tape. He is embarrassed by publicly expressed sentiment. I think he feels it's important to his job as a law enforcement official to never show any emotion unless it's the kind of emotion that results in a criminal breaking down and confessing to a crime. Also, we live in Minnesota, where emotion hibernates for the winter and then leaves town during the summer.

"Dad! I'm so happy to see you," I said.

I could tell by the way he looked at me that he was happy to see me, too, but I wouldn't expect him to do anything bizarre like for instance say it out loud. He has his own way of saying things, and in this case he expressed the tender emotions he was feeling simply and directly: "Who the hell is that weird looking girl?"

He was pointing at Cinderella, who was standing behind me and nervously looking behind her to see if our pursuers were catching up with us.

"She's my new friend," I said.

"You know I always want you to make new friends," Dad said. "But is she getting you into any trouble?"

"I've gotten her into a lot of trouble, sir," Cinderella said. "And I'm very sorry for that. But right now I'm trying to get her out of that trouble."

"Dad, how did you get here?" I asked.

"I'm not exactly sure," he said. "It's a little hard to explain."

I knew what he meant. I didn't know how I was going to explain the weird things that had happened to me, but now that Dad had entered into the weirdness, it might make things a little easier.

At this moment, Strepgoat galloped into view. I don't think my dad had ever seen a half-man/half-goat before — I mean, come on, until recently, I never had either — so it wasn't surprising that he looked at the partially anamorphic doctor with deep suspicion.

"Okay, now, who, or what in God's name are you supposed to be?" Dad said, glaring at Strepgoat.

"I'll field this one," I said. "He runs an illegal detention facility and he kept me prisoner against my will."

It took Dad all of two seconds to push him against a wall and handcuff his front two hooves behind his back. Strepgoat tried to kick back with his hind legs, but it was no use: Dad had encountered much worse. This was probably the first time Dad had ever busted any kind of centaur, but Strepgoat was receiving the exact same treatment a single-species assailant would get.

"I'm a licensed psychiatrist!" Strepgoat called out in protest. "*A licensed psychiatrist!*"

This did not hold any sway with my dad. If anything it was a mark against Strepgoat; Dad didn't think much of the psychiatric profession, although to be honest, it wouldn't hurt him to talk to a therapist once in a while, and by once in a while, I mean every day.

Concretia and the Prince arrived. I think they had been counting on Strepgoat to do the dirty work of arresting and restraining Cinderella and myself. But Strepgoat was the one being arrested. So Concretia and the Prince just stopped and looked at the intimidating figure of my dad, not quite knowing what to do.

"You, sir," the Prince said, addressing Dad in a wavering voice that had all the bravado of a grandmother making a bake sale announcement on a public address system. "What is the meaning of this? Are you some sort of Sentry?"

My dad gave the once-over to the Prince, who still didn't have a hair out of place, which only made him seem more suspicious, and Concretia, whose concrete hair, on the other hand, was beginning to develop potholes. I think Dad had thought that Strepgoat was going to win the award for the strangest sight he had seen all day, but now he was starting to realize that there were many more contestants in this category.

"So who are these two supposed to be?" Dad said.

"That dude tried to marry me, and she's his accomplice," I said.

It took an even shorter time for Dad to frisk and cuff the Prince and Concretia, although when he tried to see if she was hiding any contraband in her hair, he hurt his hand and decided to save that particular search for a later time when he would have access to a pic and shovel.

Cinderella was watching all this in a state of agitation, the kind of jumpy, nervous state that set off alarm bells in my dad's emergency alert system of a brain. I don't think Dad quite trusted her yet, but I'd forgotten that he already had a fairy tale character in his life.

"I've been working with this weirdo who helped me find you," Dad said, pointing at a figure in the darkness behind him. "I didn't believe a word he said at first, but then he managed to open up this trans-dimensional whatchamacallit from inside our basement, so I decided I had no choice but to..."

Dad didn't get a chance to say anything more, because Agent O had come up from behind and whacked him over the head with a blackjack. I screamed as Dad fell unconscious to the floor. Agent O removed Dad's pistol from his holster and pointed it at us.

"It's back to the reformatory for both of you," he said.

Oh, yeah, right. In all the excitement, I had forgotten that Agent FG had already told us that Agent O was her accomplice.

The time had come for Cinderella and I to admit that our escape was not going well.

CHAPTER TWENTY-ONE

Not only did we end up back in the reformatory, but Dad, Cinderella and I were taken to a section I had never been to before. It was a big holding pen in the middle of an even bigger room. We were surrounded by steel bars, and a dozen Sentries stood on the other side of the bars facing us.

Cinderella paced the cell while I sat next to my dad, who was lying unconscious on the floor. I was really worried that he had been seriously hurt by the blackjack.

"Dad, wake up, please wake up," I kept saying, as if that would make any difference. But then he began to groggily return to consciousness. His head started to move and his eyes slowly opened.

Then he sat up with a start. I know Dad likes to be in control of things, but for a split second he had no idea where he was or what was going on.

"The hell..." he growled.

"Dad! We're in jail in the fairy tale reformatory. You were hit on the head from behind by that ogre, and..."

"Yeah, that big jerk sucker punched me. I remember now," he said.

He stood up and pretended to not be in pain, which is a specialty of his. I could tell his head was still hurting, but he wasn't going to give his enemies the satisfaction of knowing this. That is so my dad.

He marched over, wrapped his fists around the steel bars and addressed the Sentries, who just continued to stare back at him with their guns drawn, trying to conceal that they were afraid of him despite their superior fire power.

"Who's in charge here?" Dad demanded. "I want to talk to your superior officer. I'm here to tell you that what you are doing is illegal and you're all going to be in big trouble unless you let us out of here."

The Sentries did not respond. They just continued to stand at attention, showing no emotion. This gave me the thought that the authoritarians in charge didn't seem to ever have disciplinary problems with the men in this fairy tale kingdom, just the women. I guess that's because in a society where men make the rules, men are more likely to benefit from conformity, so they are quicker to embrace it, whereas women are prone to think outside the box because in most cases they're not allowed inside the box.

It's a theory anyway, and it lead me to a deeper question — why the hell was I spending my time coming up with theories about gender issues when I should have been figuring out a way to break out of this freaking jail?

Dad didn't seem to have any good ideas at that moment, either. It looked like he was going to bang on the bars, but then he thought better of it. Dad is tough and prone to outbursts, but he also likes to maintain his composure. He tries not to ever do anything that isn't helpful to his situation and he knew that banging on the bars was not going to help anybody.

"I'm so sorry, dad," I said. "This is all my fault."

"No," he replied. "I'm the one who let down my guard. I knew that I shouldn't trust the ogre guy, but when he opened up that hole in our basement wall and we entered this goofy alternative universe or whatever the hell it is, I figured maybe he knew what he was talking about."

"Is it okay if I ask how he opened up the portal?" Cinderella said.

"Of course it's okay," Dad replied. "It's a good question."

"I just don't want to get on your nerves," Cinderella said.

"Everybody gets on my nerves," Dad said. "But if my daughter says you're okay, then you're okay with me. Laura doesn't have nearly the number of friends that she deserves. So if you're her friend, fine, I'll cut you some slack, even though you're from a fairy tale world that from what I've seen so far is one of the worst neighborhoods I've ever patrolled. But my one requirement is that you never do anything against the law."

If Cinderella had been drinking a beverage at that moment, she would have done a spit-take. "I'm afraid we've broken every conceivable law in this place, sir," she said.

"The laws in this world don't count," Dad said. "They're the laws of a totalitarian state, not the democratic state where I live and work. Anyway, to answer your question, when Laura called me up on the phone from this place, the ogre got on the line with some girl that put him to sleep."

"Dronezzz," Cinderella said.

"Well, whomever he was talking to, he fell asleep. He insisted beforehand that I not wake him up, and even though the whole thing was screwy, I went along with it. Later, when he woke up, he told me that during his sleep he was able to astral project. He claimed he flew invisibly into this prison and found out the code that opened up the trans-dimensional portal. I think he knew how to get here the whole time, but first he wanted to commiserate with his accomplice."

"Agent FG," I said. "I saw her talking to herself, but now I know she was communicating with the ogre while he was astral projecting."

"Whatever he did, the end result was the wall in our basement opening up. We then traveled through the tunnel to this alternate universe. If the landlord ever finds out about that portal, he's going to double our rent, the bastard."

"I know, I thought about that myself," I said.

Anyway," Dad said. "Here we are."

"Here you are indeed," came a voice from outside the cell. It was Agent FG. Agent O was also there, and Strepgoat was clip-clopping alongside them, like they were his new best friends.

"I don't know who you are or what you're into," Dad said to Agent FG. "But I'm going to throw the book at you."

"You have no book to throw at us," Agent FG said. "But your daughter is going to be part of a book, the storybook that tells the Cinderella story."

"What are you talking about?" I said.

"You'll be happy to know that your wedding to the Prince is going forward as planned," Strepgoat said.

"I don't want to marry the Prince!" I said. "I'm not even going to give him my phone number."

"She's too young to get married!" Dad said. "I would never allow her to even date that nimrod. He's a loser."

"Don't worry, Mr. Police Detective," Agent FG said. "Your daughter and the Prince will not be sharing any intimacies. They're just going to have a beautiful wedding, be pronounced man and wife, and then, after the words 'and they lived happily ever after' are entered into the storybook, you, your daughter, and Cinderella will be done away with. You won't exist in this world, or any other world for that matter."

"This is crazy," Cinderella said. "Why are you making her go through with the marriage? It's a sham, it's not real."

"Yes, agreed, it's all a fairy tale," Agent FG said. "But she fit into the slipper so she has to be the one the Prince marries. Once we get the formalities over with, we'll kill you all off and then the kingdom can remain in its enchanted state until we need another Cinderella."

"The mistake we made last time was trying to lobotomize you before the wedding," Strepgoat told Cinderella. "That was too upsetting for your friend. Too bad, because if she had just gone along with everything, she'd be safe at home by now and this ordeal would be over."

"Yeah, well, here's the thing," I said. "I wasn't about to stand by and allow you to hurt my friend. I'm a little new to this whole friendship thing, but I think that would have been a lousy thing to do."

"I'm proud of you, honey," Dad said. "And none of that matters because I am shutting down this storybook. I see a fairy tale character, I incarcerate the son of a bitch! You hear me!"

Agent FG just laughed, but Doctor Strepgoat was freaked out. I could see it in his face and also in the poop that was dropping to the floor from his goat-butt.

"You have no power or jurisdiction to do anything like that," Agent FG responded. "The laws of your world do not apply to this world."

"Whatever, I'm am not marrying the prince," I said. "You can't make me!"

"Oh, I can't?" Agent FG said. "You forget, my dear. I'm a Fairy Godmother."

She took out a wand and waved it. The next thing I knew, I was wearing a different and more elaborate sparkly gown, with a tiara, and dazzling jewels all over me. What made it all somewhat less than enchanting was the slight inconvenience of me now being covered in chains that were wrapped around the length of my entire body like UPS packaging tape.

It was difficult to move my arms and legs. I knew this because now I was walking. The magic wand had transported me to outside the cell and now Agent FG, Agent O, Strepgoat and several Sentries were accompanying me — slowly — back towards the main section of the reformatory.

"Here comes the bride," Doctor Strepgoat sang.

"The bride almost just stepped in your goat turds," I said, and he immediately became angry at me for reminding him of his continence issues. Good!

I turned and looked back at Dad and Cinderella, who were still in the cell.

"Dad?" I said in a pleading tone.

Now he was banging on the steel bars, as pointless as that was.

"We're going to get you out of this mess! I promise!" he said.

I wasn't so sure.

CHAPTER TWENTY-TWO

Okay, this was the worst wedding ever, and not just because it was my own forced arranged marriage and I was wearing chains and I didn't want to get married and my dad and my best friend were in jail and we were all going to be killed afterwards.

You know what, on second thought, the reasons I just gave are exactly why it was the worst wedding ever, but I couldn't deny that this was an occasion I'd remember for the rest of my life (because my life would be over soon).

The ceremony was being held in the cafeteria. It was still decorated the same way it had been for the Prince's brunch, except now there were paper flowers strung along the walls. This was supposed to make everything seem more elegant, but it basically felt like I was being married at Arby's.

All of the girls from the reformatory were seated in rows of chairs as I walked down the aisle, and many so-called dignitaries were in the VIP section in front of them. I was being led by Strepgoat, who I guess was "giving me away." Agent FG and Agent O were walking right behind us, the worst bridesmaids of all time.

The reformatory girls all had the kind of expressions on their faces that would get you thrown out of a funeral parlor for being a bring-down. At first I assumed their sad demeanors were due to their jealously over my marrying the Prince. But the resentment they held encompassed much more than a single incident. It was a lifetime of being trapped in a story someone else had written, and they were not happy about it, especially since their unhappiness was essential to that story. I don't care who you are, nobody wants to go through life being a plot device.

I arrived at the end of the aisle, where a large scroll, the size of an IMAX movie screen, had been set up.

The musicians were standing at attention. When we arrived at the end of the aisle, Strepgoat gave them the signal and they lifted up their horns and played that one short fanfare song they know. (Honestly, being a musician in the fairy tale world must take a whole hour of study and practice.)

When they finished playing the fanfare, there was an awkward silence. Apparently the Prince was expected to enter the room at that second, but he didn't. Instead, after a few more painfully quiet moments of coughing and rustling in chairs, another Witch, dressed in regulation witch-garb, entered the room carrying a magic wand. She addressed the gals.

"The Prince is not happy with how unhappy all you girls are," she said. "So I have been authorized to cheer you up and bring some much needed magic and enchantment into your lives."

She waved her wand and the orange jumpsuits of every reformatory girl were transformed into sparkly gowns that made their previous sparkly gowns look like potato sacks. I've never seen clothes sparkle and glimmer like this before; it was dazzling to the point where it hurt your eyes.

But this did nothing to improve their moods. They had been transformed from depressed prisoners in orange jumpsuits into depressed prisoners in dazzling sparkly gowns. There was now an overall misery in the room that fashion could not placate.

Strepgoat took note of the sour looks on everyone's face. "This is outrageous!" he said. "This is the happiest day of the Prince's life. And now you are being given the opportunity to experience happiness the only way any girl can ever expect to experience it: vicariously."

If he thought this was going to result in a sudden Disney Princess Cruise of joy, what he got instead was a roomful of girls getting their Sylvia Plath on.

"This is a moment to celebrate and be positive," he continued. "That is why I feel quite confidant saying on the Prince's behalf that you bitches can all go to hell!"

At that moment the musicians lifted their horns and played their entire musical repertoire: that one fanfare ditty. The Prince entered the room with a regal self-confidence that was as grating as it was unearned. And even though he was wearing a crown, the only phrase that popped into my head was "asshat." He was smiling and prepared to accept the adulation that was his due simply because he had been born.

But none of the girls clapped, and the VIPs gave him only a half-hearted smattering of applause, although to be fair this was them at their most enthusiastic. A lack of passion and an inability to feel anything is what had made them such Very Important People in the first place.

But the Prince had embraced cluelessness as a lifestyle choice. He was smiling the kind of smile you only see on the faces of privileged dudes after they've killed an endangered species. "Let us begin," he said.

Agent O grabbed me and rotated my body so I was standing next to the Price and looking in the same direction. Agent FG waved her wand, and these words appeared on the giant scroll:

"Do you, Prince of the Fairy Tale Kingdom, take this fair maiden to be your lawfully wedded wife?"

Underneath this text was written the following:

"1 – I do."

"2 – All of the above."

Strepgoat handed him a huge feathered pen and the Prince wrote a checkmark next to "1."

Then Agent FG waved her wand again and another message appeared on the giant scroll. It read:

"Do you, the Designated Cinderella, take the Prince to be your royally wedded husband, to worship and obey, and continue worshiping and obeying forever and ever for all eternity or until you meet some sort of untimely demise in the near future?"

And then underneath this, it read:

"1 – I do."

"2 – Warning: It would not be advisable to answer any other option but 1."

Agent FG waved her wand yet again. The huge feathered pen appeared in my hand, and some unseen force moved my hand towards the scroll. I was seconds away from writing a checkmark next to "1," totally against my will.

A spell that forces you to write might actually be a good thing for a writer, maybe that would explain Stephen King's incredibly prolific output, but in this case I tried to mentally fight back against it.

"Wait a minute!" I said. "When is the 'speak now or forever hold your peace' part of the ceremony?"

"We don't do that around here," Strepgoat said.

"But doesn't anyone have anything to say? Doesn't anyone want to speak a few words?"

I turned my head and looked around the room. My eyes hit upon the one girl who I thought might be able to help me.

"Dronezzz, step forward and say something," I said.

Dronezzz stood up and stepped forward.

"Oh, no you don't," Strepgoat said. "No! No! No! No!"

But Dronezzz had already started talking. "Why doesn't this wedding have a vegan option?" she asked. "I think one of the reasons my energy is so low is because of my blood sugar. Now, veganism as it relates to blood sugar is a fascinating topic…"

And I was fast asleep. I figured they couldn't make me get married if I was unconscious. Could they? Yeah, they probably could. But at least I was able to astral project and check in on Cinderella and my dad.

CHAPTER TWENTY-THREE

As I astral projected and floated unnoticed in my sleep-state into the cell block, I saw to my surprise that Concretia was there. I didn't see her at the wedding and it was my guess that she was upset that the Prince had gone back on his promise to make her his new Cinderella (I called it!). The Sentries were all keeping a watchful eye as Concretia stood not far from the steel bars, addressing Dad and Cinderella.

"It's not fair! It's so not fair that the Prince picked your daughter over me," Concretia was saying to my dad.

"Hey, I got news for you, honey, life isn't fair, not in this world, not in my world, not in any world," he replied. "So what are you going to do, just sit around and whine all the time?"

"I've had it worse than most," she said. "I've had to go through life cursed with this concrete head of hair. It's made me a freak!"

"We're all considered freaks in this place," Cinderella said.

"I know, and the powers-that-be just keep doing whatever they can to make us feel like freaks," Concretia said, turning to my dad. "Even non-freaks like your daughter are taught to feel like a freak."

I didn't know how I felt about her calling me a non-freak. That's a strange thing to hear when you're drifting between time and space without any bodily form. I seemed pretty freaky to me.

"I know now that the Prince is never going to make me his Princess," Concretia said. "I'm never going to fit in on their terms; I can only fit in on my terms. So I've come to the conclusion that when you live under such repression, you have to either be yourself or go crazy."

"And which way are you going to go?" Cinderella asked.

"Oh, I've decided to multi-task," Concretia said. "I'm doing both." She abruptly banged her head against the steel bars. The force of her concrete hair was like a wrecking ball hitting the cell, and several of the bars fell apart, leaving a big enough space for Dad and Cinderella to fit through.

Of course, the Sentries went nuts, but Concretia turned, swung her hair, and knocked several of them over. This had more of a bowling ball effect than a wrecking ball effect because several of the Sentries fell into other Sentries, making them tumble to the floor.

By this time Dad had gotten out of the cell. He grabbed one of the muskets from one of the Sentries and started hitting several of the other Sentries with it. I don't think he was even hitting them that hard, but they all immediately fell to the floor, as if an actual confrontation with violence had made them suddenly decide to become pacifists and protest violence. Sometimes the threat of physical harm can really bring out the Gandhi in a person.

But some of the Sentries were still comporting themselves like pony-tailed euro-trash trying to take over Nakatomi Plaza. And Cinderella was punching, kicking and karate-chopping every one that came at her. She had some sick Kung-Fu moves that totally contradicted her reputation as a submissive waif, which I guessed was why this particular set of skills was not emphasized more in the storybooks.

I started to think about how stories for little girls are often manufactured by a patriarchal publishing industry, but then I got slapped in the face. Not by the patriarchal publishing industry, or even one of the Sentries. It was Doctor Strepgoat.

"Wake up! Wake up," he said, and I was awake, back in the cafeteria where the wedding was taking place.

"Nice try getting Dronezzz to talk to you so that you'd fall asleep and miss the wedding but we took care of that!" he said, pointing to Agent FG, who was holding Dronezzz tight with her hand over her mouth. She was trying to speak but her voice was muffled. I could barely make out the words "keto diet" and "lactose," but she wasn't being clear enough to put me to sleep.

"Let the wedding proceed," the Prince said, as bright and cheerful and punch-in-the-face-worthy as ever.

But at that moment, Dad, Cinderella and Concretia burst into the room. They were all carrying muskets. Dad ran up to the alter, knocking down a few more Sentries along the way, and pointed his weapon straight at the Prince.

"I said I forbid you to marry my daughter and I meant it!" he said.

Cinderella came over and undid my chains. And even though my nose wasn't itching, I immediately scratched it, just because I could.

"This is now a shotgun wedding," my dad told the Prince. "Meaning, if you don't end this wedding I will blow you away with this shotgun!"

I felt very close to my dad at that moment, but then I realized there was something else of Dad's that was even closer to me: his gun. Agent O was holding it directly against my head.

"I am going to shoot your daughter with your own gun," Agent O said. "Put down that weapon or the Prince will be a widower before he even marries."

That made no sense, but Dad had already started lowering his musket. He wasn't about to let me die this way.

Concretia was standing not far from us, and I could see that Lunchabelle was not far behind her.

"Concretia," she said. "Whose side are you on now?"

"I'm on the side of all us girls. I'm on the side of freedom and individuality. I'm on the side of resistance!"

"You sound like Cinderella now," Lunchabelle said.

"That's right," Concretia replied. "Everyone wants to be Cinderella. Well, I've learned that anyone can be Cinderella!"

Wow. It sounded like Concretia was on the cusp of a profound truth.

"You heard me," she continued. "It is within us all to be Cinderella. As long as we're willing to kick dudes in their testicles."

Uh, okay, maybe she needed to workshop that profound truth and flesh it out a bit.

But Lunchabelle was open to the point Concretia was making. "Food for thought," she said. "Resistance is about being free, not just gluten-free."

Wow. In my opinion, the profound truth Lunchabelle came up with was way more bumper-sticker ready than Concratia's.

"You know what?" she added. "You've given me a really fun idea."

"What's that?" Concretia asked.

"Let's riot!"

And that's exactly what they did. Every girl in the place lunged at the nearest Sentry, witch, dignitary, VIP, and authority figure.

And the sudden commotion distracted Agent O for a moment, so I was able to step on his foot, and knee him in the groin, so I guess I had taken Concretia's words to heart, but this was a situational action, not an overall philosophy I was embracing.

As the Ogre doubled over in pain and dropped to the floor, Dad ran over to me, grabbed his gun, and said, "Okay, let's get out of here!" Then he turned to Cinderella, "Show us the way!"

We dodged flying objects and falling Sentries as we ran to the spot where the trans-dimensional tunnel was. It was still open.

"Come on, Cinderella, let's go!" I said.

"You and your dad go on ahead," she said. "I'm staying here."

"What?"

Cinderella then said the worst thing she'd ever said to me:

"This is goodbye."

CHAPTER TWENTY-FOUR

"Come on, Laura, let's get going!" Dad said. "I wouldn't mind staying here and closing this operation down, but my first priority is to get you to safety."

But I didn't want to go back without Cinderella.

"Why is this goodbye?" I said, as the riot continued to rage behind us.

"My work here isn't done," she said. "The resistance has only just started. Even if we overthrow this reformatory, there are other more powerful forces in the kingdom that will try to maintain the same polices of the Prince."

At that moment I could see Strepgoat, Agent FG and the Prince fending off the girls who were in the process of trashing everything. They helped Agent O to his feet and headed for the exit. It looked like they were getting away.

"Look!" I said. "They're escaping! I'll help you get them!"

I started to move out of the portal and back into the Reformatory, but Cinderella grabbed my arm and stopped me.

"No," she said. "You have to go back to your own world. This is not your battle."

"She's right, sweetie," Dad said. "Hell, I'd grab those jackasses right now and bring them back to our realm to be put on trial, but the laws of our world don't apply to fictional characters, so they'd just be let go and extradited back here anyway."

"I finally have a chance to escape from the Reformatory," Cinderella said. "But it would be wrong for me to run away into your world; I have to run back to my own world, and then I can lead the resistance against this regime. It's what I've been wanting to do ever since I was thrown into this joint. And now I'm going to make it happen. And I owe you a huge debt of gratitude for that."

"But... But I was hoping you'd stay with us, we can totally put you up in our house," I said, my voice cracking. "I really like having you as my friend."

"We'll still be friends," she said. "But you live in the real world, where it's okay to be care-free and have fun. I live in the fairy tale world, which as you've learned is a living hell."

"Why can't life be less like a fairy tale and more like life?" I said, tears streaming down my face.

"I know, I know," Cinderella said, hugging me tight, not caring that what I was saying didn't make much sense. That's how good a friend she was.

I could tell Dad was impatient to get moving, but he wasn't rushing me either.

"You've been a good friend to Laura," he said to Cinderella. "I wish she could meet more people in her school like you, but let's face it, most teenagers are idiots."

My dad was being sweeter than usual, but what he said next totally took me by surprise.

"Laura's mom would like you a lot if she were still alive. You and Laura are both the kind of smart, strong woman that she was."

It was so odd and wonderful to hear him say that because Dad never talked about my mom, ever.

"I used to read your story to Laura at bedtime," he said to Cinderella.

"You did?" I said. I had no memory of this.

"Yes, when you were a little girl."

"You read storybooks to me?"

"Sure. All the time."

"All the time?"

"Well, once. At your mother's insistence. That's why I know you lost your mom as well, Cinderella. And I bet if she was alive she'd be just as proud of you as Laura's mom would be of her."

Cinderella now did the boldest thing I had ever seen her do. She stepped forward and gave my dad a big hug. Nobody ever hugs my dad. I do sometimes, but not often enough, so I also stepped forward and hugged him, too.

I know Dad appreciated this moment, but it took him about two seconds to become embarrassed and self-conscious about the whole thing.

"Okay, okay, we'd better be going," he said.

"Yeah," Cinderella said. "I love talking to you guys, but I've got to go be a riot girl."

"Will you keep in touch?" I asked.

"Of course!" Cinderella said.

She turned around and started heading back to the Reformatory, but then she turned back gave me one last look.

"If you want, there a way you can keep tabs on me," she said.

"How's that?"

"In storybooks! Keep an eye out for the next revised edition. It's going to be action-packed. Oh, that reminds me, I still have your iPad."

She walked back towards us and handed it to me.

"Thanks," I said. "I'll give the next edition of your storybook a four star recommendation." Then I thought better of it, and added, "Uh, or maybe I'll just give you my review in person."

Cinderella smiled, turned around and rejoined the riot. The last thing I saw was her battling several Sentries, kicking ass and not taking names (this was no time for paperwork).

"Laura?" Dad said as we stared to head further into the tunnel. "Did you just almost forget to take your iPad back home with you?"

"Uh, yeah, I guess."

He shook his head disapprovingly. "It's not like you to be so careless."

We weren't even home yet and things were already starting to get back to normal.

CHAPTER TWENTY-FIVE

Dad and I returned to our house. The moment we entered our basement, the cosmic passageway closed behind us. In the tunnel, we had felt lost for a while, but then we ran into Zombie Anna Karenina, who helpfully pointed us in the right direction. Apparently, the author of Vampire's Weekend WIth Zombies has written a new book where Anna Karenina becomes a Walking Dead Countess after her train mishap. I'll have to give that one a read. Uh, maybe.

Of course, neither of us could forget what we had just seen or where we had just been, but Dad insisted that the thing to do now was return to our normal life.

"It's going to take me a long time to get over not being able to throw those deadbeat criminals in jail," he said, referring to the Prince, Strepgoat, Agent FG, Agent O and the other fairy tale perps. "But there's plenty of justice to pursue right here in the good old U.S.A. so I'm going to focus on that."

And what was I to focus on? My continuing education, of course. I had just escaped from a soulless institution that tried to crush my spirit, so it wasn't all that big a change of pace when I went back to school the next morning.

(This whole adventure had taken place over the course of a single night. Was it all a dream? For the record, just to be clear — no, it wasn't a friggin' dream!)

My first morning back was uneventful. At lunchtime, in the cafeteria, nobody was rioting, so I was bored. It occurred to me that the time had come for bold action. I was sitting in my usual solitary spot at the moody loner table when Gil Davis – you know, *the* Gil Davis – entered the room. I decided to be brave and take the extraordinary action I had always been meaning to take.

I made eye contact with him.

Yes, I understood the magnitude of the risk I was taking. But I was sick of living my life in a straitjacket. Screw it. I was going to make eye contact with this guy even if it meant a potential noontime apocalypse.

And so, Gil Davis walked past me and I looked at him and met his eyes.

You heard right, I looked at him. I wasn't messing around.

And then, in a startling development, he looked at me.

And this lead to something neither of us expected: we looked at each other.

Things were getting out of control.

There was looking, looking back, more looking, and still more looking back.

Freak show!

And then, just when it seemed like things couldn't get any freakier, Gil Davis talked to me.

You heard right. Talking. Actual verbal communication. I hope those of you who take Ritalin are not off your meds because I realize this is some kinetic, 3-D, CGI, surround sound THX-level stuff I'm talking about.

"Hey," he said.

Hey," I replied.

We were off to a good start, but the conversation went even further from there.

"What's up?" he said.

"Not much, what's up with you? I replied.

"Not much," he said.

Okay, now we were getting somewhere. But it was up to one of us to articulate things to the point where we could move forward.

"Wanna hang out?" he said.

"Sure," I replied.

"Cool," he said.

Then we both just stared at each other, him hovering by my table, me looking up from my tray of nutritiously pointless food. It was strange and awkward, yet it felt nice. Now that I had taken the bold step of talking to him, it seemed okay to just stare into his green eyes (yes, they were green, I now had confirmation). There was an alternate universe in those eyes that I wanted to get lost in.

But at a certain point, something more had to be said. So I said the first thing that popped into my head:

"Wanna dance?"

"Sure!"

I'm fully aware that it's not normal for a girl to ask a guy to dance, even less so when you're in the middle of a school lunchroom in a building that houses a system dedicated to the principles of conformity and conventionality. And for someone who used to do everything she could to avoid attracting attention, this was just plain out-and-out craziness. Which is why I was happy to be doing it.

I stood up and faced him and started to dance.

"There's no music playing," he said.

"So?"

He had no answer to that, but even better, he didn't seem to want to have an answer to that.

So we danced. In the middle of the school cafeteria. To music that we were both hearing in our own heads that might have been completely different, but somehow seemed to rhythmically synch.

Everyone was staring at us and snickering and I was entering into legend as the biggest weirdo nerd geek in the history of the Minnesota public school system. But I didn't care. My dancing was decidedly dorky, and I wasn't even waltzing. Still didn't care. We were having a good time and we could have lived happily-ever-after just dancing like that forever, or at least until the bell rang, but then the teacher monitoring the cafeteria, an uptight middle-aged man who had just turned thirty, came along to put an end to the madness.

"You're causing a disturbance in the school cafeteria!" he said. "You've got three days detention, missy!"

Wow. I had a date *and* detention. It felt so cool to finally have a social life.